A Candlelight
Ecstasy Romance ™

HIS LIPS WERE WARM, MOBILE, AND SEARCHING.

Within seconds they had drawn all resistance
from her. Her arms slid up to cling to his
shoulders, as if she might fall if she let go. His
mouth moved on hers slowly, penetrating more
deeply, and she felt his arms tighten around her
and was aware of the hard demand of his body.
Yet even then she did not pull away. In the end it
was Thorne who stepped back, holding her at
arm's length and breathing unevenly, his eyes
searching her face.

"What are you trying to do?" he said with a
touch of harshness. "Turn the tables on me? You
are supposed to set the limits. You'd better
remember that, Rhea."

CANDLELIGHT ECSTASY ROMANCES™

Web of Desire

Jean Hager

A CANDLELIGHT ECSTASY ROMANCE™

Published by
Dell Publishing Co., Inc.
1 Dag Hammarskjold Plaza
New York, New York 10017

Dell ® TM 681510, Dell Publishing Co., Inc.

Candlelight Ecstasy Romance™ is a trademark of
Dell Publishing Co., Inc., New York, New York.

ISBN: 0-440-19434-2

Printed in the United States of America

First printing—December 1981

Dear Reader:

In response to your enthusiasm for Candlelight Ecstasy Romances™, we are now increasing the number of titles per month from two to three.

We are pleased to offer you sensuous novels set in America, depicting modern American women and men as they confront the provocative problems of a modern relationship.

Throughout the history of the Candlelight line, Dell has tried to maintain a high standard of excellence, to give you the finest in reading pleasure. It is now and will remain our most ardent ambition.

Vivian Stephens
Editor
Candlelight Romances

For my fellow "romantics"—
Delores, Fran, Suzan, Lois, Renee, and Genell,
faithful friends and discerning critics

Chapter 1

The snow, which had fallen steadily since she was an hour out of Oklahoma City, swirled thickly against the windshield. With the wipers going full speed, Rhea strained against the seat belt, peering intently ahead into what appeared to be a wall of white that continually moved forward with the car, just beyond the reach of the headlights.

What was normally less than a five-hour drive had taken more than seven hours. She was approaching Idabel, still ten miles from the cabin, and it was growing dark. If she had not stopped in McAlester to have tire chains installed, she doubted that she would have made it this far.

Close to a foot of snow must be on the ground now and the rate at which it continued to fall did not seem to have abated even slightly. An unusually heavy amount of snow had already been dumped on southeastern Oklahoma, and the storm was shaping up to be a record-breaker. In an area unaccustomed to and ill-equipped for so much snow, the digging out could take days.

It was for this reason that Rhea did not allow herself to succumb to her weariness and the small town's inviting lights, pale shimmering haloes viewed but dimly through the whiteness. Leaving the settlement reluctantly behind, she turned off the highway and started up the narrow road leading to the cabin. Absently moving her head from side to side in an effort to ease taut neck muscles, she kept her gaze on what she could see of the road ahead; and her booted foot remained firmly pressed against the accelerator.

She became aware that her leather-gloved fingers were numb from the unconscious pressure she had been exerting on the steering wheel, and she forced her hands to relax.

The mountain road had begun to curve and climb steadily. A narrow, serpentine track, it was bordered by densely growing trees—pine, oak, hickory, ash, and red maple—that at the higher elevation beyond the cabin became the Ouachita National Forest.

This was Choctaw country, the place where her ancestors had lived since the early 1800s, the scene of her childhood and teen years. And even though she had spent only a few weeks a year here since her college graduation almost five years earlier and her parents and grandfather were no longer living, it was still "home" to her in a way that no other place had ever been.

That was why she had kept the cabin that had been Thorne's wedding gift to her. But she could not think of Thorne now, although his unexpected appearance at her Oklahoma City apartment was the reason she had fled the city so precipitously in the face of the approaching storm —fled as if all the hounds of Hell were close on her trail.

The rigid self-control she had learned during the past few years had stood her in good stead on the drive. That and the necessity of giving the road her undivided attention had made it possible to keep thoughts of her estranged husband pushed back into the shadowy reaches of her mind beyond consciousness. There would be time enough to deal with painful memories when she was safe inside the snug cabin.

The track became steeper. As she carefully negotiated the near-hairpin curve that she remembered as being about a half mile from the cabin, the car began to slide sideways. With surprising presence of mind—but this would not occur to her until later—she tapped lightly on the brake pedal and swung the wheel into the direction of the slide.

Her quick reactions kept the car upright, but the solidly frozen undersurface of the road prevented the tire chains from gaining enough purchase to keep the vehicle on course. She sat helpless as the car slid, nose first, into the shallow ditch alongside the road and jarred to a stop against the trunk of a towering, snow-blanketed pine.

Fortunately her seat belt prevented her being thrown against the steering wheel. After a single fearful groan and a few moments to assure herself she was unharmed, she took stock of her situation and realized the only thing left to do was to proceed to the cabin on foot.

She released the seat belt and reached for the pile-lined wool coat that had been tossed from the seat to the floorboard when the car left the road. She put it on over sweater and skirt, pulled up the hood, and buttoned the front opening all the way to her chin. She took the flashlight from the glove compartment and transferred her suitcase from back seat to front. Because the car was leaning toward the passenger side, it was difficult to get the driver's door open. She finally accomplished it by pushing with both feet.

Then she scrambled out, retrieved her suitcase, turned on the flashlight and slammed the door behind her. She climbed back up the shallow incline to the road, her high-heeled leather boots sinking inches deep into snow.

Back on the track, the beam of her light picking out the steep lane between the trees, she walked as fast as the snow and the uphill grade would allow. Within moments she was gasping for breath, the cold air burning in her chest. She forced herself to slow down. She couldn't risk a twisted ankle in this isolated spot, at night with the temperature dropping steadily. She should be grateful, she told herself grimly, that the wind was at her back.

It seemed ages before she trudged around another bend in the road and her flashlight beam picked out the cabin back in the trees, looking small and cozy with pale yellow light shining from one of the front windows.

Sharp relief rushed through her now-shivering body, for the light could mean only one thing. The Sinclairs, a retired couple who lived in a larger cabin a mile farther along the road, had been able to carry out her telephoned request to lay in a supply of groceries and firewood before the snow made a trip into town impossible.

For the past four years she had paid the couple a small monthly sum to keep an eye on the cabin, clean it occasionally, and make any necessary repairs. When she'd spoken to Maggie Sinclair early that morning, Maggie had assured her the cabin would be ready for her. With the reticence of one who guarded her own privacy, Maggie had not even admitted to curiosity about the unscheduled January vacation.

The snow had started in the central section of the state two hours later and, in spite of Maggie's reassurances, Rhea had not been able to help feeling somewhat anxious, fearing that the Sinclairs might have put off the trip to town until too late. But she should have known they were as good as their word—hadn't they always been?—and, as she made her way through the trees and up the cabin steps, her last trace of anxiety was erased. A large stack of firewood filled half of the front porch to one side of the door.

She found the right key and, with the help of the flashlight, unlocked the door. Inside she dropped her case and leaned back against the door while she caught her breath, feeling somewhat like a small, hunted creature who has managed with its last bit of strength to elude its pursuers and find a safe, dry place to rest.

She sighed and looked about the main room of the cabin. When she had come into possession of it, it had contained nothing but a rickety table and a sturdy iron bed. She had furnished it gradually over the past four years with pieces found at auctions and garage sales. She had taken night classes in furniture refinishing and upholstering with the result that she had managed to create an attractive colorful retreat.

Her gaze swept from the small kitchen and eating area at one end of the room to the stone fireplace, where red corduroy armchairs flanking a red, brown, and beige striped couch were drawn up close to the hearth. The Sinclairs had left the kitchen light on and Rhea switched on more lights as she moved about. Jake Sinclair—bless him—had even laid tightly rolled newspapers, kindling, and logs in the fireplace.

Rhea wasted no time in finding matches, for the cabin was numbingly cold. Very soon she had a roaring fire going. The other two rooms, a bedroom opening off the fireplace end of the main room and its adjoining bath, were warmed by small propane wall heaters fueled by a line from a tank behind the cabin.

Rhea lighted the two heaters and returned to stand in front of the fireplace until she felt warm enough to remove her coat. With the most pressing requirements taken care of, she could no longer ignore the hunger pangs grumbling in her stomach. She tugged off her soaked boots and stockings and removed the wool skirt that was wet around the hem. She found jeans and a pair of thick knee-high socks in her case and put them on with the bulky coral-colored sweater she had worn all day.

She made a grilled cheese sandwich and heated canned chicken-noodle soup and water for instant coffee. Checking the cabinet and refrigerator more thoroughly while the soup warmed, she was reassured to find food enough for two weeks or so. There was no phone in the cabin, but she felt sure Jake would be down to check on her tomorrow and she would ask him to phone for a wrecker. But it could well be a week before the wrecker could make it out to pull her car from the ditch. At another time the knowledge that she would probably be confined to the cabin for a week might have been cause for alarm. Under the circumstances, however, the isolation gave her a feeling of protection.

She arranged the sandwich, soup, and coffee on a tray, which she carried to the couch. By that time she felt ravenous and made quick work of the meal. Then, her feet tucked under her, she curled into a corner of the couch with her mug in both hands and sipped the hot coffee while she gazed into the blazing log fire. A metal basket on the wide stone hearth held enough firewood to last the night, so she wouldn't even have to go as far as the covered porch until morning.

She was safe here. The Sinclairs were only a mile up the road if she should need them. But she wouldn't, of course. No one but the Sinclairs and her boss, Don Cragmont, at the historical society, knew where she was. And they had promised not to reveal her whereabouts to anyone. Don had even offered to say she was out of town working on a "research project" for the society if he were pressed for information.

Don, of all people, could be depended on to keep her secret, she reminded herself as she gripped the coffee mug tightly. She stared at her slender ringless fingers and, in an odd flash, saw her gold wedding band resting in its velvet-lined box in a dresser drawer in her city apartment. She had not even looked at the ring in four years, and she did not want to see it or to remember any of the emotional confusion and pain that had characterized those brief days with Thorne.

She had never sought a divorce, certain that a legal action would expose her to the glare of publicity that surrounded everyone and everything connected with the internationally known Choctaw novelist, Thorne Folsom. She had suffered through weeks of insistent phone calls and brash doorstep encounters with reporters when she left Thorne. But finally, with both Thorne in New York and Rhea in Oklahoma City persistently refusing to make any comment, they had left her alone to fade back into obscurity. She had returned to using her maiden name, Rhea Pitlyn, and hardly anyone connected her with the famous novelist anymore.

She drained the mug and placed it next to the couch on the earth-toned Navaho rug. She felt extremely weary and knew if she didn't get ready for bed immediately she would soon be too sleepy to do so. She was tempted to stretch out on the couch in front of the fire, but she would wake later, chilled, when the fire burned down.

Sighing, she got up, put more logs on the fire, turned out all the lights but the one in the kitchen, and took her suitcase into the bedroom. The freshly made-up bed was turned down—more of Maggie's doing. She found a gown in her case, got into it and, pulling out the combs that held her shoulder-length black hair away from her face at the temples, brushed halfheartedly before switching out the bedside lamp and crawling into bed. She pulled the sheet and heavy layers of blanket and comforter up to her chin.

She closed her eyes and sought oblivion in her earlier drowsiness, trying to shut out the memories that were crowding in now. Had it been a mistake to come here to the cabin that had been Thorne's wedding gift to her? He had stood in front of the fireplace that warm September afternoon, the day after their wedding, and handed her the deed made out in her name alone.

"I want you to have it so that, no matter what happens, it will always be yours." Had he known, even then, that the marriage was doomed?

The thought, of course, hadn't even occurred to her at the time. She had stared at the deed and then into the darkly rugged face of her husband with tears in her eyes before she flung herself into his waiting arms.

"Oh, Thorne, darling! I love you so!"

He had looked down at her, his brown eyes passionate and deep. "Do you?" he asked softly. Then he lifted her and carried her into the bedroom. "Show me, Rhea. Show me how much you love me."

The late afternoon sun filtered by the surrounding trees fell through the window across their bodies as they undressed slowly, savoring the anticipation of what was to come. With hands and lips and murmured endearments they brought each other to a sensuous arousal so overwhelming that, when it crested, Rhea thought she would drown in its tide.

In that moment she had been certain that no two people

18

had ever loved so deeply as she and Thorne. As she had lain curled sleepily in his arms, her body tingling with the warm afterglow of their lovemaking, she had thought that nothing could ever come between them. They had slept for a while, then made love again—in the same bed where Rhea now lay alone, staring into the darkness and listening to the soft splash of snow against the window beside the bed.

Restlessly she turned on her side, clutching a pillow against her breast. She had not counted on the memories being so strong after all this time. Perhaps she should have been warned by the shock that had rocked her to the depths of her being yesterday afternoon, the shock caused by that fleeting glimpse of Thorne waiting on the walk outside her apartment. She could not even remember driving on past and parking two blocks away. What she did remember was sitting with her head bent over the steering wheel and every nerve in her body trembling. She had thought that four years was enough time to heal her emotional wounds. But the mere sight of Thorne had shaken her so badly that she had panicked and run away. She had spent the night in a hotel, phoned Don to arrange time off from her job, and slipped back to her apartment at dawn to pack a suitcase.

She couldn't see Thorne again until she had had time to think things through and steel herself for the inevitable confrontation. She had known that in time he would want a divorce. She wanted that final step behind her, too, but she fervently wished it could have been accomplished through their lawyers. It wasn't Thorne's way, of course, to pay someone else to perform distasteful chores in his behalf. No matter how unpleasant the prospect, he had always insisted on facing situations head-on. Even now—after the shock of betrayal and the intervening years—she

19

had to admit that Thorne Folsom had his own code of honesty. He had never lied to her about himself or his past, except perhaps by omission. In fact, in retrospect, she could see that he had tried to warn her against becoming involved with him. But she had refused to listen.

She sighed and turned on her back. Touching a finger to her cheek, she found it wet with tears. How utterly naive she had been when she met him, just turned twenty-two and fresh out of the University of Oklahoma with a degree in history and a brand new job as Indian archivist with the Oklahoma Historical Society.

She had been on the job for only two weeks when Don Cragmont, editor of the society's publications and head of the library and archives, called her into his office.

"We're going to have an autograph party, Rhea, and I'm putting you in charge of the arrangements."

The society had hosted previous autograph parties for authors of nonfiction books relating to Oklahoma history. From what Rhea had heard, the head librarian, a plump middle-aged widow, Clare Rutledge, always made the arrangements. In fact, Clare had told her that she enjoyed it and Rhea was surprised to be given the chore after only two weeks on the job.

"All right, Mr. Cragmont. I'll do my best."

He made an impatient gesture with one hand. "I thought you agreed to call me Don. Everyone else around here does." He was about thirty with reddish brown hair, hazel eyes, blunt features and a ready smile that made him look even younger than his years. He smiled at her now and added, "When I tell you the name of the man we're honoring, you'll understand why I'm assigning this to you, rather than Clare. The author is Thorne Folsom."

"Oh!" Rhea experienced a stirring of anticipation. Thorne Folsom's first novel, published three years earlier, had been a critical and commercial success. His new novel, the story of a search for personal identity by a young half-breed Choctaw, had been selected by several book clubs, optioned by a movie company, and was presently moving up on the best-seller lists. *The New York Times* review of the novel had called it "a profound and illuminating story full of insight into an Indian's mind and soul and the tragedy of his alienation from his culture." Folsom, like Rhea, was a Choctaw, which explained Don Cragmont's decision to put her in charge of the autograph party.

"Do you know him?" Don asked now.

"Only by reputation," Rhea said. "I've read his books, of course."

"I know you're from the same part of the state, and I thought you might have known him before he became successful." He shrugged. "Well, it would have been nice if you were already acquainted, but I'm sure you'll have a lot in common nonetheless. Folsom's making a national tour to promote his new novel. I understand he's scheduled to be in Oklahoma for two weeks—he'll be visiting relatives in addition to pushing the book. We've scheduled our autographing for July tenth. That's less than a month away. Do you think you can handle it, in addition to your other duties?"

"Yes," said Rhea without hesitation. She had loved Thorne Folsom's books and was quite in awe of his talent. The assignment excited her, and she would do everything in her power to make the party a success.

The author was scheduled to arrive in Oklahoma City the afternoon of July 5. Rhea phoned him at his hotel that evening. He had, of course, already been informed of the autograph party at the Historical Society Library, but she wanted to tell him of the specific plans she had made and ask if he had any further suggestions.

His voice, when he answered, had a quiet steadiness about it that she had noticed in his television interviews, as if he did not find it necessary to speak assertively to be heeded. There was such self-assurance in the voice that Rhea experienced a slight sinking sensation, and for a brief moment she had the dreadful feeling that he would find her careful plans woefully inadequate.

She covered her uncertainty by saying, "We're from the same part of the state, Mr. Folsom. People in McCurtain County are extremely proud of your success."

The quiet voice took on a trace of interest that had not been there before. "Are you Choctaw?"

And when she told him that she was, he said, "Look, I think we could discuss the plans for the autographing better face to face. Have you had dinner?" He was not deterred when she said that she had. She was soon to learn that Thorne Folsom was not often easily deterred when he wanted something. "Why don't you come to my hotel for a drink then? Can you meet me in the lobby in an hour?"

She changed her dress three times before she settled on a turquoise jersey sheath with a V-neck and elasticized waist. It looked attractive without being too dressy. The only piece of jewelry she wore with it was an Indian necklace with a single turquoise stone surrounded by a scalloped edging of hammered silver.

She left her apartment, telling herself sternly there was nothing to be nervous about. Famous people were merely people after all, and Thorne Folsom was only a man like any other.

When she reached the hotel, she had another attack of uncertainty. What if she didn't recognize him? She had only seen him twice briefly on television. In the event, she had nothing to worry about. She entered the lobby to find a number of people milling about. She did not at first see the novelist. Her gaze swept over the people standing at the accommodations desk and then made a slow survey of the adjoining blue-carpeted area.

Suddenly she became aware of a man watching her across the room. He was standing near the bank of elevators and, for a moment, their eyes met and locked. Rhea had the oddest feeling—as if that moment was somehow momentous in the scheme of her life. Yet she had never met this man before and would not be likely ever to see him again after the autograph party.

His deep brown gaze traveled from her face down to her sandaled feet and back again. The look was frankly appraising with a hint of challenge, and something told her he was accustomed to sizing up people with one look and usually accurate in his judgments of them. He was tall and lean, his black hair falling casually across his forehead and overlapping his collar in back, his tan features almost harsh in their angularity. There was something in him—some galvanic quality—that had not come across on the television screen and that shouted sex appeal.

Her boyfriends from college days were just that—boys and no more than friends. She had no knowledge of experienced men-of-the-world, but some basic feminine instinct that she had not even known she possessed told her that women in general, and she in particular, held few mysteries for Thorne Folsom.

This certainty caused her to feel embarrassment and chagrin and she was grateful for the creamy tan of her complexion, which was capable of hiding the blush she felt burning in her cheeks.

They moved toward each other at the same moment and met in the middle of the blue carpet. "Rhea?" Although inflected as a question, it was more a statement of fact.

She extended her hand and said politely, "Hello, Mr. Folsom."

He took her hand in his big, hard one and continued to hold it moments longer than politeness required. His smile was warm. "It's a pleasure meeting you." He dropped her hand finally. "I've reserved a table in the club. It's this way." His fingers cupped her elbow and he steered her toward double doors beyond the elevators.

After asking her preference, he ordered wine for her and Scotch for himself. Their table was in a corner of the room with a filigreed screen forming the third partition of the private cubicle. The screen cut off much of the light from the room's large chandeliers, creating a soft dimness in their corner.

"Now," he said when their drinks were placed before them, "tell me what you've planned for the autograph party."

She did—in some detail—but although his dark eyes remained fixed on her face as she talked, she had the impression he wasn't really interested in what she was saying. Perhaps in an effort to impress him, she finally said, "The governor and several state legislators are coming over from the capitol and all three TV stations will be covering it."

His dark brows rose. "I'm impressed," he said with a cynical intonation. "But, of course, no politician would miss a chance for free TV coverage."

"If there are any suggestions you would like to make—" Her voice trailed off.

"It sounds fine," he told her. "How long have you worked for the historical society?"

"Five weeks," she admitted.

He grinned crookedly and leaned toward her, his elbows on the table. "They must think highly of you—trusting you with the governor and the legislature."

She smiled faintly. "I got the assignment because I'm Choctaw."

He laughed outright at that. "Naturally. And it's a stroke of luck for me."

"Why?" she said, truly puzzled.

Thorne Folsom sobered and said with a trace of mockery, "Come now, you know what I mean. You're a beautiful woman and I'm a normal healthy man."

Rhea's cheeks burned and her tentative poise crumbled. She had been so wrapped up in Thorne Folsom the author, she had forgotten his reputation as a womanizer. "If you approve of the plans I've made, there's nothing left to discuss. Thank you for the drink. I—I'd better be going."

She stood and started to leave the cubicle, but before she could he was beside her, his hand gripping her wrist, pulling her forward toward him, slightly off balance, so that she looked up at him with quick alarm.

"There's no need to go off in a huff, Rhea."

"I—I'm not in a huff. Would you please let go of me?"

The dark eyes held a wry gleam as he looked at her, but he did not release her. "How old are you?"

Grudgingly she said, "Twenty-two."

He stared deeply into her eyes for a long moment. "Well, this is a first."

"What are you talking about?"

"You are the first truly innocent twenty-two-year-old woman I've ever met. I'll admit I had some vague notion of having a five-day fling with you while I'm here, but I see from your outraged expression that it would be unwise to pursue the thought. I misjudged you, and I apologize." Abruptly he released her.

His frank admission stunned her and, for a moment, she stared at him without reply. She must not, she told herself, allow her discomfiture to create a strain between them. It would make the times they would have to be together during the next few days too uncomfortable—for her, anyway.

He was turning to move back to the table as she said, "I'm sorry if I overreacted. It's just that you took me by surprise."

He turned to face her again. "I surely can't be the first man to have ideas about you." He shook his head slowly. "Where did you attend college—an all-girls school?"

She tried to match his own careless tone. "I graduated from OU. You seem to have the mistaken notion that coed campuses are the scene of constant sex orgies! Well, there may have been some of that going on, but not among my friends."

"Indeed?" he said dryly. "I don't know why, but I'm glad to hear it. I wish I could hang around for the day you really become a woman."

No man had ever talked to her as Thorne Folsom was doing, and she didn't know how to handle it. She was sure another type of girl could have passed the whole thing off with a breezy comeback and a laugh. But Rhea could not find any appropriate words. There was a thick silence between them, an expectant waiting, as if the wrong words could bring about disaster. He was still challenging her, Rhea realized. She had a strong impulse to run, but she knew she had to retreat with some of her dignity intact or their next meeting could be even worse than this one.

She said, trying for a light touch, "It's probably just as well. I'm sure you'd be disappointed."

"I don't think so."

"You don't know anything about me, Mr. Folsom."

"I sense things, Rhea. I knew when I heard your voice on the telephone that you would be young and pretty. I also suspect you aren't as uninterested in me as you would have me believe. I'm getting very good vibrations right now."

She took a deep steadying breath. "Gracious, you're taking a lot for granted, considering we've just met."

"Am I?" he said mockingly and grinned at her.

He was flirting outrageously, but not seriously—more as if it were a conditioned reflex, and she resented it. She tilted her head to one side. "This conversation is really rather silly, isn't it? Don't tell me this is how you reduce all those women to jelly?"

He smiled faintly. "Do I do that?"

She shrugged carelessly. "If one can believe the gossip sheets."

"But you don't? I wonder about that." He took a step forward and, sensing his intention, she was shocked into paralysis. His arms reached for her, drawing her effortlessly against him. "This is for all those OU men who let you get away," he said huskily and then, while she stared up at him, mesmerized, his mouth came down on hers.

His lips were warm and mobile and searching, and within seconds they had drawn all resistance from her. Her arms slid up to cling to his shoulders, as if she might fall if she let go. His mouth moved on hers slowly, penetrating more deeply, and she felt his arms tighten around her and was aware of the hard demand of his body. Yet even then she did not pull away. In the end it was Thorne who stepped back, holding her at arms' length and breathing unevenly, his eyes searching her face.

"What are you trying to do?" he said with a touch of harshness. "Turn the tables on me? You are supposed to set the limits. You'd better remember that, Rhea."

27

"Did you think you could frighten me?" Rhea's heartbeat sounded like thunder in her ears as she returned his look without wavering. She was issuing her own challenge now, and she knew it. It was the first time she had felt such heady daring, and she knew it was due to her sudden realization that, under certain conditions, a woman could have power over a man.

"I don't know what I thought," he drawled. "But I know what I'm thinking now, and believe me you had better not push me any further or you might regret it. I don't think you're ready for someone like me, Rhea. Take my word for it and run along home."

She felt insulted and crushed by his sneering tone. She said hotly, "Don't worry about me, Mr. Folsom. I find you utterly resistible!"

"You're pushing me, Rhea." He smiled tentatively. "But maybe you're not even aware of it, so I'm going to ignore it."

She was searching for a scathing reply when a woman's voice behind her made her whirl about.

"Thorne, I've been looking everywhere for you! You might have let me know where you were going."

The woman who had come into the cubicle was a tall, willowy brunette in her early thirties with golden cat's eyes and a classically beautiful face marred slightly by a hint of hardness about the mouth. Her gold gaze flicked over Rhea and then she moved to Thorne's side, her slim fingers running along his bare muscled forearm in a caressing gesture. "Who's this, darling, one of your cousins?"

"This is Rhea Pitlyn from the historical society," Thorne said coolly. "Rhea, I'd like you to meet my agent, Diane Lowery. Rhea and I were discussing the plans she has made for the autograph party."

"Oh, and I interrupted, didn't I?" inquired Diane with an apologetic, but somehow seductive, smile for Thorne.

"Not at all," Rhea assured her. "We're finished."

"Good," said Diane, continuing to smile dazzlingly at Thorne. "I was getting awfully bored all alone in the room. I thought you might take me out somewhere for dinner."

"I know an excellent restaurant not far from here. Will you excuse us, Rhea?"

Rhea said, "Certainly." She forced a tight smile to her lips. "Nice meeting you, Miss Lowery. I'll probably see you at the autograph party."

"You surely will," Diane caroled as Rhea walked away and made for the double doors leading to the lobby.

As she hurried toward the hotel parking garage and her car, she found that she wanted to look back over her shoulder to see if Thorne and his agent had come out of the hotel. But she resisted the impulse. She knew even then that seeing the two of them together would be painful for her.

She was not quite sure at that moment what had happened to her in the hotel, except that a whole range of unfamiliar emotions had been awakened in her and she felt confused. She had been kissed many times, but never before tonight had she felt on the verge of losing herself in pure sensation.

That night she hardly slept at all. She lay awake and thought of Thorne Folsom and that shattering kiss. And sometimes she thought of Thorne with Diane Lowery and there was a sharp ache in her midsection, as if a knife were being twisted inside her.

Rhea came back to the present abruptly, passing the corner of the sheet impatiently over her wet cheeks. What a fool she had been not to have recognized on that first meeting that Thorne and she were worlds apart, much too far apart ever to find any kind of happiness together.

But wasn't that like asking that a child understand that fire can be painful when he has never been burned? At twenty-two without any real experience of men, she had been unable to resist the attraction Thorne held for her from the first moment she set eyes on him. Her profound sensual awakening along with the aura of danger that she felt in Thorne's presence had been too much for her to handle with any degree of maturity. She had, in fact, rushed headlong into the danger without any conception of the hurt that awaited her.

It had been a dreadful way to learn the caution of adulthood, and perhaps she had even gone too far to the other extreme. Don Cragmont, whom she had dated occasionally during the past year, had told her she had built a barrier around herself and her emotions that no man could penetrate.

Yet despite her hard-won aloofness, that brief glimpse of Thorne the previous afternoon had caused such a flood of pain and loneliness in her that she had been unable to face him. She wondered now if her reaction had been caused by the changes she saw in him. He had looked older, thinner, with a haunted expression about his deep-set eyes that had not been there the last time she had seen him.

Perhaps this should not have surprised her, for his last two books had not lived up to the promise of the first two. He had gone to Los Angeles to write the screenplay for the tremendously successful second novel, the one that had brought him to Oklahoma City four and a half years earlier and into Rhea's life. He had stayed on the West Coast for two years, living—if the stories in the scandal sheets were true—the libertine existence of the fast Hollywood set.

His work had suffered, and the critics had not been kind. Thorne Folsom had already done his best work, they said. They described him as a "burned-out" artist who, like too many before him, had succumbed to the lure of tawdry commercialism.

Knowing Thorne, Rhea could imagine how those jibes must have lacerated his pride. This had been there in that one glimpse she had had of him yesterday—an uncharacteristic vulnerability that had shattered her carefully constructed defenses. Yet their relationship had been over before Thorne had gone to Los Angeles, leaving her with nothing but disillusionment.

That disillusionment, she thought, as she turned restlessly in the bed, had been as much her fault as Thorne's. Sighing, she gave up her efforts to sleep and, tossing back the covers, got out of bed. She put on her velour robe and scuffs, then went into the kitchen to heat milk for a cup of chocolate.

She carried the drink to the couch and built up the fire again before settling back to sip the steaming chocolate and stare into the leaping orange flames.

Chapter 2

Yes, she told herself, the blame for her disillusionment rested squarely on her own shoulders. She sipped the chocolate and closed her eyes to squeeze back more tears.

After that first meeting in the Oklahoma City hotel, she had not been able to put Thorne out of her mind. The next day on the job she had gone about her duties in an abstracted state, hardly hearing when her co-workers spoke to her. Her mind had been turning over schemes to bring about another meeting with Thorne before the autograph party.

About one, Don found her in the microfilm room, where she was working on the compilation of a new index.

"We may have a problem, Rhea."

She looked up from her yellow pad. "What kind of problem?"

"The Folsom books haven't come in. According to the publisher, they were mailed to us ten days ago. They should have been here by now. Will you see if you can run them down?"

As he left the room her heart sank. It was Thursday and the autograph party was scheduled for the coming Monday afternoon. What if the books didn't arrive in time? But they had to, or she would have a new batch shipped air freight from New York. She wasn't going to let anything mar the first autograph party she had organized.

She phoned the city's main post office and asked them to make a search for the books. They agreed to put out a tracer if the parcel could not be found. She then called the airlines for a schedule of New York to Oklahoma City freight flights arriving in the next three days, in case she had to arrange for another shipment.

Late that afternoon a post office employee called to say they had not found the books and were attempting to trace them. Rhea hung up and tried to think of something else that could be done to insure there would be three hundred of Thorne Folsom's books at the library on Monday.

It occurred to her that the author might know the best person to contact at his publishing house to get things moving. She reached for the telephone again, but her hand hesitated on the receiver. It was almost quitting time and she had to drive by the hotel on her way home. She would stop and talk to him. She could leave a message with the desk clerk if he was out.

Driving toward the hotel a while later, she started to have second thoughts. She should have telephoned. Down deep, she knew she had decided to go to the hotel because she wanted to see him again. Belatedly she realized that he was shrewd enough to discern her deeper motive, and her impulsive decision suddenly seemed a transparent ruse.

The tall, clean-lined hotel loomed on her right, and pushing aside her doubts, she made the turn and entered the parking garage. There was no reason in the world why

33

she shouldn't ask for Thorne's help in rounding up enough books for his own autograph party, she told herself.

She entered the hotel lobby through an enclosed passageway from the parking garage. After the July brightness of the street, the lobby seemed dim. She hesitated briefly, then approached a house telephone that sat in a wall niche near the accommodations desk. She was about to dial Thorne's room when someone called to her from across the lobby. She replaced the receiver and turned to see Diane Lowery coming toward her.

The brunette, dressed in an expensively tailored cream linen suit with matching pumps, looked as if she'd just stepped off a page in *Vogue*. Her smile was as cool as her outfit. "Miss Pitlyn, isn't it? What are *you* doing here? Thorne didn't mention anything about an appointment."

"There's no appointment," Rhea said quickly. Diane Lowery's calculating golden eyes made her feel flustered. "I—there's a problem with the books and—I thought Mr. Folsom might be able to help. I—I was on my way home from work and stopped on the off chance I might catch him in."

"Oh, I'm afraid you're out of luck. He left his suite some time ago. I'm sorry but I have no idea when he'll be back." Rhea had the oddest feeling that the other woman not only knew when he'd be back but where he had gone. Well, she couldn't hang around the hotel and wait for him to return, at any rate.

She said carelessly, "It doesn't matter. I can phone him tomorrow morning. He might not be able to help me, anyway."

The agent smiled briefly. "He probably won't, you know—be able to help you, I mean. Thorne is totally uninterested in the less creative aspects of publishing and promoting his books." Her tone was amused and indulgent. "He has the artist's disdain for anything but his writing. That's why I'm accompanying him on this tour, to take care of things like that. Why don't you tell me your problem and I'll see what I can do."

Rhea could hardly refuse without seeming rude, if not irrational. "The books haven't arrived, although they were shipped ten days ago. As a last resort, I can have a new shipment sent by air, but then if the others show up I'll have twice the number we will probably need. I thought Mr. Folsom might know whom to contact at the publishing company in New York."

Diane Lowery laughed. "My dear, he wouldn't have the vaguest notion. The marketing division isn't even housed in the same building with the editorial offices. However, I know the local distributor. He'll run this down for you. Why don't I call him first thing tomorrow morning and get him working on it?"

"If you're sure it isn't too much trouble—"

"It's part of my job. I'll contact you tomorrow at the historical society as soon as I know anything."

"Thank you," said Rhea, frowning slightly. "I'll have to order the air shipment before five tomorrow, if it comes to that."

"Don't worry," Diane said breezily. "I'll handle it. The books will be here by Monday morning at the latest. You have my personal guarantee."

"All right. Thank you again."

The agent's gaze ran over Rhea shrewdly. "I'd better be off. I have an appointment and I've a taxi waiting. May I give you a lift?"

"No, thanks. My car's in the hotel garage."

"Good-bye then." The other woman turned on her elegant spike heels and strode across the lobby toward the main entrance. Just before she exited, she glanced over her shoulder, causing Rhea to flush guiltily and move hastily toward the door leading to the parking garage. Before she reached it, she heard the elevator doors opening and hesitated long enough to see Thorne Folsom crossing the lobby, heading for the club.

Rhea didn't move for a moment, unable to believe it was really he. Hadn't Diane Lowery said, or at least implied, that he'd left the hotel? Had she been mistaken, or had she deliberately lied?

Before she had time to think about all the possible consequences, Rhea turned around and, almost running, followed him across the lobby, catching up with him at the doors leading into the club. Looking round, he saw her and stopped.

His dark brows rose in astonishment. "Rhea! I'm surprised to see you here. Don't tell me I've forgotten an appointment."

"No, you haven't." She was relieved to hear her voice sounding so cool and collected. "I was going to call your suite. I've run into a problem getting your books and I thought you might help me."

He smiled, but the narrowed eyes held a perplexed expression. "I will, of course—if I can."

"It isn't necessary now. I just saw Miss Lowery and she says she can take care of it."

"Good. Diane's very efficient." He studied her with a contemplative look. "I was about to have a drink before dinner. Will you join me?"

Rhea realized that her intercepting him, after his agent had already said she would get the books, must look as if she were angling for an invitation. "Thank you—but I must be going. I stopped here on my way from work."

"Do you have another engagement?"

"No," she admitted.

"I have an even better idea then. Will you have dinner with me? Someone told me about a new restaurant over on Tenth. We can walk from here."

"Well—" She suppressed a feeling of unease. "I'd like that very much." She glanced from his open-collared beige silk shirt and crisply pleated brown trousers to her simple blue cotton dress, which was a little rumpled after her day's work. "If you think this dress will do."

His eyes wandered over her, hesitating momentarily on the curving outline of her breasts. "It's fine."

Outside on the sidewalk, he thrust both hands into his trousers' pockets and they walked at a leisurely pace. "How long have you been away from Oklahoma?" she asked, more to have something to say than because of any great interest in the answer.

"I've lived in New York for almost two years now. It's more convenient being near my editor and agent. I've made some good contacts in the publishing world since I moved there. Sometimes the crowds and the traffic get to me and I wish I were back in Oklahoma. Not this way, though."

She glanced at him, puzzled. "What do you mean?"

He shrugged slightly. "I don't really like autograph parties and interviews—all the hype. Diane assures me it's a necessary evil if I want to get my books in the hands of great numbers of people. But that doesn't mean I have to like being promoted—like toothpaste or dental floss."

She smiled. "Miss Lowery warned me you were not interested in anything but your writing."

"That isn't strictly true." Amusement twinkled in the eyes that held hers, and she felt her cheeks grow warm. "There are one or two things that I like even more than writing." She looked away from him and he said, "We turn here. The restaurant's half way down this block."

37

It was called Frizbee's and the interior was an informal melange of paneled walls decorated with brass planters trailing ivy and small gold-clothed tables with chairs upholstered in gold velvet. Although it was early, many of the tables were already occupied, and an appetizing smell that seemed to be a mixture of grilled steak and freshly baked bread hovered in the air.

They were shown to a table next to a window overlooking the street. Thorne held her chair. When he sat down opposite her, she saw that his expression was thoughtful.

"This is nice," Rhea said, glancing about. "Lucky for me I saw you. Otherwise I'd have been eating a sandwich at home."

"I was told the veal cordon bleu is good." He was watching her with undisguised speculation, as if he did not believe she had merely met him by accident, but rather had been waiting for him to appear. Unfortunately this was near enough to the truth that Rhea did not care to offer a defense. "That sounds wonderful."

He told the waitress what they wanted, ordering wine before the meal. Then he leaned back in his chair and said lazily, "You mentioned you were on your way home when we met. Where is that?"

"An apartment complex out on Pennsylvania Avenue."

"You live alone, of course." This was said with a hint of mockery.

"Yes." Her mouth felt suddenly dry and she picked up her wineglass and sipped slowly, enjoying the cool tang of it in her mouth. She cast about self-consciously for something to say. "Are—are you working on a new book?"

"In my head—there's nothing on paper yet. It looks as if I'll be offered a chance to write the screenplay for the last one, and if I decide to do it the work on the new book will probably be postponed for some time."

"If!" Rhea was astonished that he didn't seem excited over the prospect of doing a screenplay. "But that sounds marvelous! You aren't considering turning it down, are you?"

He shrugged carelessly. "I'm still deliberating. I'd probably have to move to the West Coast. That's not all bad, although Diane keeps telling me my career will suffer if I leave New York."

"She doesn't think you should do the screenplay?"

"She wants me to do it in New York—with an occasional trip out to Los Angeles. I'm not sure that would work. I'm not even sure I could do justice to the screenplay. It's a totally different type of writing."

"But wouldn't you enjoy the challenge?" she persisted.

He gave her an amused glance. "I prefer to choose my own challenges. Don't you? Yesterday I would have said you prefer to avoid challenges altogether and play it safe. Now . . ."

"I find my job challenging," she told him a little defensively. "Of course it's still very new and I don't think I would want to be an archivist indefinitely. I'm not sure what I'd like to do later on. It would be nice eventually to work at something that I felt was more of a contribution to the world."

"You have ideals, do you?" She realized that he was teasing her and it irritated her.

"Yes. What I really wanted was to go to law school so that I could help poor people—Indians and other minorities. But my parents are dead and there wasn't enough money for anything beyond my baccalaureate degree."

He grinned. "Somehow I can't see you as a lawyer. Ah, here's our food."

The cordon bleu, served with green beans almondine, was delicious, and although Rhea found her companion's refusal to take her seriously somewhat disconcerting, she was hungry and enjoyed the meal. She turned down dessert and Thorne said, "Perhaps you'll feel like coffee after our walk back to the hotel."

They strolled idly back the way they had come. Once Thorne's bare arm brushed warmly against her own, causing an incursion of electric excitement along her veins. She glanced up at him under her dark lashes and saw his face set and still. Yet, incredible as it seemed, she sensed that he was as aware of her as she was of him. The knowledge gave her a heady feeling of triumph that stayed with her all the way to the hotel.

In the lobby he said abruptly, "We'll go to my suite and have the coffee sent up."

Looking back later, she would realize that that was probably her last chance to retreat, the last real opportunity she had to turn away from the dangerous attraction Thorne held for her, go back to her safe, if narrow, life and forget him. If she had refused the invitation to go to his suite . . .

But she hadn't. She smothered her qualms and rode up in the elevator with him in a strangely tense silence. At his door, he fitted the key into the lock and ushered her into the air-conditioned coolness ahead of him. Then he told her to make herself comfortable while he phoned room service.

The suite consisted of a sitting room and a bedroom that could be seen through an open door. Rhea, who by that time was feeling nervous and on edge, sat down in a green brocade armchair that stood at right angles to a curving beige velvet sofa. She glanced about surreptitiously for a sign of feminine occupancy, for it had suddenly occurred to her that Diane Lowery might be sharing the suite with him.

A man's brown terry robe was thrown across the foot of the bed in the other room. She could see it through the open doorway. She saw nothing that suggested Diane might be sharing the suite, but she didn't know whether to be relieved by that or not. From where she was sitting, she could view only a small portion of the bedroom and nothing of the bath. But surely Thorne wouldn't have brought her there if Diane might be likely to walk in at any moment.

When he'd hung up, he came over to sit on the sofa. By that time, Rhea's nervousness was beginning to verge on panic. What was she doing in Thorne Folsom's hotel suite? And how could she leave now without making an utter fool of herself? He was watching her with an interested expression. She stirred in the chair and said, "I—I hope room service doesn't take long. I have to leave in a few minutes."

"Why?" he inquired. "I thought you said there was no one waiting."

"There isn't. I—"

He smiled lazily. "You're having second thoughts about coming here. Right?"

"I'm not in the habit of going to men's hotel rooms," she said primly, twisting the silver ring on her right hand in an agitated gesture.

"That's fairly obvious," he observed with heavy irony.

"Is—is Miss Lowery's room on this floor?" She could have bitten her tongue the moment the words were out, for his short laugh told her he knew precisely what thoughts she had been entertaining about his relationship with Diane.

"She's not staying here, so you needn't worry about her walking in on us unannounced. She's next door." He indicated an interior wall of the sitting room. There was a

41

connecting door, Rhea noticed and thought derisively, *Very convenient!*

"I didn't think she was staying in your suite," she protested.

"Of course, you did," he said curtly.

A waiter from room service arrived then. Thorne brought a tray into the room and poured the coffee, placing the cups on the low table in front of the sofa. "Come sit over here by me," he said carelessly, not even looking at her. He was being so casual, she thought, as though he did this all the time, as perhaps he did. After her blundering question about where Diane was staying, she did not want to make an issue of something so trivial as where she should sit.

She moved to the sofa, leaving a good distance between them, and picked up one of the cups. She was thankful to have something to do with her hands. The coffee tasted bitter in her mouth, however, and she drank only a few sips before setting the cup aside.

The silence seemed deafening. To break the tension, she said, "I was told you'll be visiting relatives while you're in the state. Is your immediate family still here?"

"My parents are dead," he said. "I've an aunt here in the city and a sister in Poteau. I'm driving down to see my sister and her family next week." He set his coffee cup aside and faced her, one arm resting along the back of the sofa. "Anything else you'd like to know?"

"I'm not being nosey," she said defensively. "I might be asked for some background information on you—by the TV stations."

"I see," he responded, amused. "Well, then, I'm thirty-two years old. Never been married—never even came close. I attended the University of Texas on a scholarship and took graduate work in literature at Rice. I'm in excel-

42

lent health, and in addition to my work I like golf, racquet-ball, good food—" He paused, then added in a teasing voice, "And beautiful women."

Rhea looked at him through the dark sweep of her lashes. "And they like you back, I'm sure."

"Some of them." His tone was dry. "Now it's your turn to tell me about yourself."

"I don't want to bore you."

Ignoring her reluctance, he persisted, "You said your parents are dead?"

"Yes. I've no close relatives left except for a couple of cousins in New Mexico. You know where I went to school, where I work and where I live. There's nothing else to tell."

He reached out and took her hand. "There's quite a bit more, I should say." With his other hand he touched her face, gently tracing the outline of one high cheekbone and her chin. "I find you very beautiful."

His hand had come to rest on her shoulder, sending pleasurable warmth through the thin fabric of her dress. She was amazed to realize how much she wanted him to go on touching her. She tried to keep her tone light as she said, "And you like beautiful women—I know. So you surely can't find me all that attractive since you've already told me I'm not a real woman."

"We can take care of that," he told her. "Isn't that really why you're here?" Almost before she realized what he was doing, his hand had moved to touch her throat. Somehow the top button of her dress had come unfastened. She didn't know if that was by design or accidental.

"No—" she stammered.

"You aren't going to stick to that story about running into me by accident in the lobby, are you?" He smiled derisively. His hand had found the soft fullness of her

43

breast above the sheer lace of her bra. His fingers stroked the tender skin, causing an exquisite weakness that was almost like a sigh to spread languidly through her body. She stared at him wordlessly. She had hoped to see him again, and she had desperately wanted to have dinner with him. Then, because she had been reluctant to have the evening end, she had come to his suite willingly. Perhaps it *had* looked as if she wanted to be seduced. And now, with his hands moving expertly over her body, she wasn't at all sure that she didn't. But not like this, not with Thorne thinking she was throwing herself at his head.

"Thorne—please don't." She had never before called him by his first name, except in her thoughts, and it gave an intimacy to the feeble protest that she had not intended.

He slid a hand through the thickness of her hair. His fingers pressed against the nape of her neck, pulling her toward him as his lips touched hers, tentatively at first, and then pressed hungrily. Her hand had spread itself between them in what started as a defensive movement, and now her palm was pressed against the hard muscles of his chest where his shirt lay open. The feel of his heart thudding beneath her palm ignited a flicker of desire deep inside her.

The kiss deepened with such naked longing that her other hand, as if it had a will of its own, entangled itself in the hair at the back of his neck and pressed him closer.

Her heart thundered in her ears and her lips parted under his mouth's insistence. His gasp of pleasure mingled with her own breath so that a moan of bittersweet yearning escaped her. But beyond the agonizing craving of her senses and the chaotic whirl of her emotions, she retained enough coherent thought to know that if she did not stop him, she would later regret it desperately. This was not the way she wanted to leave her girlhood behind—carried along by harsh lust without the tenderness of love.

Suddenly she pushed against him and turned her mouth away from his kiss. Her senses reeling, she choked out, "I can't, Thorne."

His breath came raggedly as he stared into her face. "What's the matter?" he scoffed softly. "Isn't this what the whole evening has been leading up to?"

She met his stony look, then turned away. "No . . ." She broke off. "I—I admit I came to the hotel tonight hoping to see you again."

"After I warned you to stay away from me, what did you think would happen?" His tone was hard and unyielding. "Did you imagine we'd have coffee and a cozy little chat here, and that would be it?"

"I don't know—I wasn't thinking that far ahead," she said helplessly.

Thorne swore under his breath. His hands gripped her arms and he told her cruelly, "Rhea, when you pursue a man openly, there is only one conclusion he can draw. I took it for granted we both had the same ending in mind for this evening. You're even more naive than I thought."

"Let me go," she said stonily. "I'm leaving."

He released her and got to his feet in one swift movement. "Yes, I think you'd better." He drew a tired-sounding breath. "The last thing I want to do is push you into something you're not equipped to handle."

Trembling, she stood and, without looking at him again, left the suite.

Years later, curled on the couch in the cabin, Rhea trembled anew just remembering that second meeting with Thorne. Belatedly, she became aware that the mug in her hands, still half full of chocolate, had grown cold as she sat gazing into the leaping flames.

She shivered and carried the remaining chocolate to the kitchen and poured it down the drain. Leaning against the counter, she pushed her falling hair away from her face with both hands. Her eyes burned with fatigue and she closed them for several moments to ease the scratchy feeling.

She wondered what she had hoped to accomplish by coming to the cabin to dissect the past once more. She had done that often enough in those first weeks after she had left Thorne. It had not changed anything then, and it certainly would not change anything now. It did no good to relive those days in her mind, but a heavy cloud of melancholy memories seemed to hover in the cabin, and she could not help thinking back, painful as it was.

She straightened and looked at her watch. It was two o'clock in the morning, still several hours before dawn. But she did not think there would be much sleep for her tonight.

Chapter 3

Restlessness drove Rhea to pace aimlessly back and forth in front of the fireplace. Finally, she went to one of the front windows and, pushing aside the rough-textured curtains, she peered at the dense blackness that pressed against the outside of the glass and listened to the lonely wind as it howled about the cabin.

That humiliating scene in Thorne's hotel suite might have been the end of it, she thought, if they hadn't been thrown together again at the autograph party the following Monday . . .

The party was a great success. So many people came that they ran out of books; all three television stations carried interviews with Thorne on the evening's newscasts. Diane Lowery, in a slinky black dress, made as much of a hit with the press as Thorne himself. Rhea thought Diane was a bit overdressed for an afternoon autograph party, but even she had to admit that the agent was as efficient as Thorne had said she was. She moved through the crowd charming the important guests—Diane seemed to have a sixth sense for picking them out on sight—and helped Rhea see that the serving of refreshments ran smoothly and that a stack of books remained at Thorne's elbow until the supply was exhausted.

Clare Rutledge took the money for the books, freeing Rhea to oversee the party. When the festivities were winding down, Diane approached the table where Thorne had been sitting all afternoon. She had a blond, bearded man in tow. His name was Ben, and his summation of the war novel he was writing had impressed Diane so much that she had invited him to dinner to continue the discussion. Evidently she was seriously considering the unpublished author's request that she represent him.

Rhea, who was helping Clare count the money so that the older woman could drop it in the bank night depository on her way home, overheard these scraps of the conversation at the table. Then she heard Diane say to Thorne, "You'll come to dinner with us, won't you?"

"I'm sure you can discuss your business better without me," Thorne said.

Diane's urging did not change his mind, and so the agent and the clearly gratified young author left the library together. When Rhea and Clare had finished tallying the money and Clare had gone, Rhea glanced at Thorne who had crossed the library to gaze out a window. Everyone else had departed.

"It's time to lock up and go home," she ventured. "Need a lift back to your hotel?"

Running a hand tiredly through his black hair, Thorne turned to face her. "The party seemed to go without a hitch. It's one of the best autographings I've ever had. You are to be congratulated."

"Thank you," she said, flushing as his eyes rested steadily on her face. "I'm glad you're pleased."

He smiled wryly. "I don't want to have dinner alone. Will you save me from such a fate?"

It occurred to her that if he disliked eating alone so much he could have gone with Diane. However, his words and actions toward her during the afternoon had been nothing but circumspect. She felt that he had decided to keep their relationship, whatever there was left of it, on a less personal footing. In fact, she was so convinced of that, she saw no reason why she shouldn't accept his dinner invitation.

"All right. Do you mind if we go by my apartment first so I can change clothes? One of the legislators spilled punch on my skirt. He was so dazzled by Diane that he evidently forgot he was holding a cup of punch and sloshed it all over the floor. I happened to be passing at that moment and some of it splashed on me. He was quite embarrassed when he realized what he'd done."

Thorne laughed shortly. "Diane is a bit overwhelming on first meeting." He left the window and came toward her. "We'll stop by your apartment and I can phone for reservations from there."

They drove in virtual silence. After offering two or three opening gambits and getting only monosyllabic replies from Thorne, Rhea gave up trying to draw him out and merely drove. She wondered if his disinclination to talk meant he was regretting his dinner invitation. But when she parked in front of her apartment and turned toward him, she saw that his head was propped against the back of the seat and his eyes were closed.

"Thorne." She touched his arm lightly.

He stirred and for an instant his dark eyes regarded her with puzzlement. Then he straightened and smiled ruefully. "Forgive me. I dozed off for a moment."

"You're exhausted. Why didn't you tell me that instead of going ahead with plans for dinner?"

He looked at her with a glint in his brown eyes. "Trying to wriggle out of our date?"

"No," she said dryly, "but you're obviously dead on your feet. You don't have to prove anything to me, Thorne."

He ignored this. "If you're going to change, hadn't we better go in?"

She shrugged and they got out of the car. Upon entering the apartment, she had a sudden impulse and said, "We could have dinner here, if you prefer. I've part of a ham. We could have it with a salad and potatoes baked in the microwave."

He was looking at her with his head cocked to one side. "I admit that sounds much more attractive than fighting a crowd in a restaurant. Are you sure you don't mind?"

"I wouldn't have suggested it if I did," she said. "You can make the salad."

He shrugged out of his suit jacket, removed his tie, unfastened the top button of his shirt, and followed her into the kitchen. "Going to make me work for my supper, eh?" he drawled easily. "Well, show me what to do."

She got vegetables from the crisper and placed them on the cabinet. She handed him a knife from the utility drawer. "There's a bowl to the right of the sink. Cut up some of each and toss them together. While you get started on that, I'll go put on something more comfortable." At the teasing grin that lifted the corners of his mouth, she forestalled any wrong interpretation of her remark by adding hastily, "Jeans," and left the room. Behind her she heard him chuckling.

A few minutes later, she returned wearing jeans and a white knit shirt.

"How am I doing?" he asked.

She glanced at the bowl of salad vegetables. "A bit heavy on tomato, but it'll do."

"Oh, is that all?" He sounded deflated. "I think this is a beautiful creation, considering that I don't even know how to make a salad."

"It's past time you learned then," she told him.

After setting the ham and potatoes into the microwave, she made coffee and put out plates and silver while he sat at the kitchen table and watched her.

"Rhea," he said suddenly, "is there anyone special in your life?"

For a moment, she stared at him, bewildered by the abrupt question. Then her dark eyes flicked away from him and she went to the refrigerator for salad dressing. "I've already told you I have no close family left."

"You know that isn't what I meant." He sounded wry. "Is there a man in your life?"

She felt warmth creeping up her neck. "I don't think I care to answer that," she said tartly.

"What about your boss?" he persisted. "He seemed particularly interested in you today."

Surprised, she gave him a startled look. "Don? Don't be silly. He was just being his usual friendly self. He's like that with everyone."

"Funny, I didn't notice that."

She set the ham and potatoes on the table and poured the coffee. Sitting down across from him she said, "Tell me about the book you're working on—the one you said is still in your head."

His mouth twisted in sudden amusement. "And mind my own business?"

"Well . . ." she said helplessly.

He raised dark brows, eyeing her, then split his baked

potato and added a generous chunk of butter. Apparently he decided to let the subject of her private life drop. "It'll be a generational saga of a Choctaw family from about 1850 to the early 1900s. I'm going to base it partly on my own ancestors."

As they ate, he talked earnestly and sometimes hesitantly, as if he were working something out as he spoke, about the book he hoped would be the crowning achievement of his career. "I don't want to start writing too soon," he told her seriously. "This one's too important. I've a great deal of research and thinking to do before I put a word on paper. I'll work on other things in the meantime, and I'll know when the time is right."

As he continued to speak, Rhea became engrossed, not only in the tale he was unfolding, but in the deep, somehow hypnotic, timbre of his voice. *He could have been an actor,* she thought, *with a voice like that.*

The meal finished, they lingered over coffee. "Diane must be very excited at the chance to represent such a book."

"I haven't told her anything about it. In fact, you're the only person I've mentioned any of this to." His glance resting on her face seemed to sharpen.

"I'm flattered."

"Yes?" His eyes skimmed over her dark hair and oval face. "You're a rare woman. You really listen when someone else talks," he said, surprising her. "That seems at odds with your obliviousness to some other things."

"What things?"

"I'm talking about Don Cragmont. He's interested in you."

Rhea lifted her coffee cup and did not answer.

"Are you?" he demanded.

She looked up. "Am I what?"

His mouth twisted as he met her eyes. "Are you interested in Cragmont?"

She set her cup down. "I told you before I don't care to discuss my boss."

"I suspect you're not interested in him in a personal way, or you would have noticed *his* interest."

"You barely know me. How can you know what I'm feeling?" His steady look made her feel self-conscious. "Besides, I don't believe in becoming personally involved with my superior on the job. That would be a difficult situation."

"Not at all. If you cared for the man you could find a way around the difficulties."

His unruffled persistence on the topic made her bristle. "Do you always make these snap judgments about people you've just met?"

The dark planes of his face hardened with some sudden emotion. "There are some things that are obvious at the first look," he said tightly. "You have a very revealing face. I watched you today with Cragmont. It was evident you had no deep feelings for him. A thing like that can't be hidden, especially to someone like me who—" He broke off.

"Who's had a lot of experience with women?" she finished, angered. "You needn't remind me of that!"

"I meant nothing of the kind," he bit out crisply. "Well, I see I've touched a nerve, and I apologize."

It was not the first time he had apologized for his rudeness and now, as at the other time, Rhea did not think he was entirely sincere. His manner was not the least bit apologetic.

She got up and began to clear the table. After a moment he said, "I was going to say that, as a writer, I've learned to observe people and their reactions. It's fuel for the imagination."

"What I do or do not feel for Don is none of your business. And I resent your using your imagination to arrive at these farfetched conclusions."

"It seems a shame, that's all, for you to bury yourself in that library. You'll end up married to some dull fellow with little notion of the depths of emotion of which you are capable."

"Let's drop it, shall we?" she snapped.

He watched her silently as she finished arranging the dishes in the dishwasher and started the machine. Then he followed her into the living room. Rhea was stubbornly determined not to break the silence that had descended between them. Perhaps sensing this, he said sardonically, "I did not come here with the intention of getting you riled up at me all over again. I meant to leave you with a better opinion of me by exerting all my charm."

She made a small bitter sound and he smiled. "I presume that means you are unaware that I have any charm."

"I just don't believe my opinion of you matters to you one whit."

"Now who is making snap judgments?"

They were still standing in the middle of the living room, and since he made no move to go Rhea was about to issue a grudging invitation for him to have another cup of coffee. She had turned slightly toward the sofa when his hands reached out to catch her shoulders. He pulled her toward him. She was too surprised to resist as his hard mouth fastened on her lips, parting them easily. His hands slid down her back to her waist and pressed her hard against him.

As on the other occasions when he had held her, she found the impact of his sexual power irresistible. Her senses stirred and came to clamoring life. She was aware of the danger, but she could not move away from it. It was like standing at the edge of a cliff and feeling an irrational compulsion to jump. She was aware, too, of the truth in Thorne's assessment of her life. The even procession of her days until now had left her untouched by passion that was so potent as to be irresistible. As his mouth gentled and moved to touch the wing of her brow, she realized that in some ways she had been dead until Thorne came upon the scene and brought her starving senses to life.

When at last he moved away she was dazed, her eyes still closed, her mouth tingling with pleasure while deep inside her there was an ache such as she had never known before.

"Good-bye, Rhea," he said huskily.

She drew a shaky breath and opened her eyes. She saw his dark face through a haze of still-reeling emotions. He was retrieving his jacket and tie from the sofa. "You—your schedule calls for you to be in Tulsa tomorrow, doesn't it?" she asked inanely.

"Yes," he said, straightening and tossing the jacket and tie over one shoulder.

"Good-bye then."

He regarded her for another moment, his expression inscrutable, and then left the apartment. Sinking into the sofa, she listened to the sound of his footsteps receding outside. She had been too confused to think of offering him a ride to his hotel. Thorne, however, would not have been shy about asking if he had wished, so evidently he preferred hailing a taxi.

The apartment seemed so empty now that he was gone. She suspected that subconsciously she had wanted him to suggest they see each other again. How else could she explain the sense of betrayal she was feeling? Clearly he did not *want* to see her again. There had been a note of finality in his last good-bye. As for Rhea, in addition to feeling let down, she felt very young and foolish, something she had not experienced in a long time. She had not felt so vulnerable since her widowed mother died during her second year at the university.

The death of her last close relative had pushed her into a maturity of sorts. There had been very little money and she had been forced to find a part-time job to provide the supplementary income she needed to finish college. There had not been a lot of time for socializing and she had told herself she didn't miss it. She had assumed an air of self-sufficiency that had hardened over the years. All of her friends believed her to be what she appeared—a reserved, independent young woman.

Now, in the course of a few days, Thorne Folsom had gotten past the mask she presented to the world. She was too inexperienced to cope with the dynamic novelist who had seen and done things she had never known. It was fortunate that he was leaving the city tomorrow, she thought. She would not see him again and, for her own good, she ought to be thankful for that. She told herself that she was.

This conviction did not keep her from moving through the following days with a vague feeling of bereftness. She had always been relatively content with her life, concentrating on her job and what passed for her social life—occasional outings with a few close friends. Now she discovered a faint but persistent dissatisfaction in herself, as she began to perceive her days as a dull procession of monotonous activities.

Late Friday afternoon she entered her apartment and, for the first time in memory, felt no anticipation at the prospect of having two days in which to do anything she chose. As she made her dinner, she began to toy with the idea of driving somewhere for the weekend. Her funds were limited, but she could afford a trip to Missouri's Silver Dollar City or the races in Hot Springs. She had reached the point of pondering which of her friends she might ask to accompany her when the telephone rang.

Thorne's deep voice at the other end sent a shock through her that caused the blood to leave her head in a rush. She lowered herself to the sofa, struggling for some semblance of nonchalance. *What's the matter with me?* she asked herself desperately. *I'm letting this man make an utter fool of me, and he is far too perceptive not to realize it.*

"Rhea, are you there?"

She gripped the receiver, feeling stupidly confused.

"Have I called at a bad time?" She heard a faint smile in the tone.

"No . . . not at all . . ." She looked around the room that had seemed so empty ever since Thorne had walked out of it on Monday night. She definitely had to get out of there for the weekend, she told herself. "Where are you?"

"I rented a car and drove over. I arrived about an hour ago."

"Here? You're in Oklahoma City?" A surge of elation —tinged with wariness—swept over her as the information seeped in. He was here and he must want to see her, or why had he called?

"Yes, I'm at my aunt's house."

"How did things go in Tulsa?"

"Well enough," he said. "I'm bushed. I'm going to shower and hit the sack early."

Her disappointment was a sharp pang. "Oh . . . well, it was thoughtful of you to call to say hello."

"That isn't why I called." Challenge had crept into his

voice now. "I'm driving to Poteau in the morning to spend the weekend with my sister and her family. I thought, if you have no other plans, you might like to come with me."

Rhea swallowed, glancing once more about the silent apartment and trying to make some sense of his request. The thought of the whole weekend spent in Thorne's company aroused desperate longings in her. At the same time, she could not ignore the warning signals the practical side of her nature was sending out. The weekend would end, and then it would be harder than ever to go on with her calm, ordinary life. And could she maintain even a shred of dignity if she should spend two full days with Thorne Folsom? It was easy enough to tell herself that they would not be alone, but staying with Thorne's sister. But it took several hours to reach Poteau by car, and she was too well aware of the effect Thorne's nearness had on her not to realize that anything might happen during those hours.

As if he could read her thoughts, Thorne said ironically, "We'll be properly chaperoned. My sister is a stickler for appearances."

"I was just wondering if I could get away," she lied brazenly. "It would be fun to see some of the places I remember from my childhood." Had there ever been any real doubt as to what her answer would be? "Yes, I'd like to go with you, Thorne."

"Good," he responded blandly. Clearly, *he* had not expected a negative reply. "I'll pick you up about nine in the morning."

It wasn't until she had hung up that she had time to be amazed at herself for agreeing to spend the weekend with him. Of course, they would be with his sister's family. She pushed her doubts aside and went into the bedroom to pack an overnight case. After that she spent the remainder of the evening shampooing and setting her hair and doing her nails. Suddenly the weekend was no longer merely a stretch of lonely hours to be filled somehow. She sensed that it could be the most important weekend in her life.

Grace Boucher, Thorne's sister, accepted the arrival of her brother accompanied by an unknown girl with perfect equanimity. After giving Thorne a fierce hug, she smiled warmly at his companion. "We're pleased that you could come with Thorne, Rhea. Are you from around here?"

"I was raised in Idabel," Rhea said.

"Why, that's just down the road," Grace remarked. A man came into the living room from the back of the house. "Here's my husband, Harold. Honey, this is Rhea Pitlyn, Thorne's . . . friend." Rhea did not miss her hesitation over the last word. Clearly Grace Boucher was wondering how Rhea figured in her brother's life.

Harold Boucher was not much taller than his wife, who was only of medium height, but he was stockily built, in contrast to her slenderness. Sharply etched high cheekbones and a generous Roman nose gave strength to his bronze face.

His welcome sounded as genuine as his wife's, which relieved Rhea of some of the uneasiness she had been feeling, for it was becoming fairly clear that Thorne had not informed the Bouchers he was bringing a guest.

Harold Boucher clapped a big hand on Thorne's shoulder. "Thorne, you old son of a gun! How are you?"

The two men moved across the living room, talking animatedly. Grace said, "Bring your case, Rhea, and I'll show you where you'll be sleeping."

Rhea followed along a hall, off which three bedrooms opened, to a room at the end. Even if Thorne had not already told her that Grace had two daughters, it would have been obvious it was a young girl's room with its canopied bed and pink-checked gingham curtains and spread. A large Raggedy Ann doll reclined against the bed pillows.

"I feel as though I'm imposing, taking your daughter's room," Rhea said.

"Lisa won't mind," Grace assured her. "She can bunk with Jody—that's short for Joanna. The girls are both so thrilled to have Thorne here they'd gladly sleep outside if necessary! They've gone to their scout meeting, by the way. They'd have skipped today, but they had to turn in the money from their cookie sales."

Rhea set her case beside the bed. "You're being very kind, especially since I suspect Thorne didn't tell you he was bringing me."

Grace laughed easily. "Well, he didn't—but I've stopped being surprised by anything Thorne does. And you *are* welcome, Rhea. To tell you the truth, I was beginning to despair of my brother's ever bringing a girl home with him. I've always known those women the gossip columnists link him with weren't important because he never mentioned them in his letters—and he never brought one home before."

As Grace talked, Rhea felt more and more uncomfortable. As soon as the other woman paused, she hastily demurred, "I'm afraid you may have gotten the wrong idea about me. I've only known Thorne a short while. We're just friends."

"Oh?" Grace was plainly surprised by the information, but she recovered quickly. "It's none of my business, anyway, and we're happy to have you with us for as long as you can stay—which, if I know my aggravating brother, won't be long."

"He plans to return to Oklahoma City tomorrow, I think," Rhea told her. "He's scheduled to be in Texas next week to promote his book. His agent has gone ahead to take care of the preliminaries."

Grace made a face. "Oh, I had hoped to keep him longer than one night, but it's no more than I expected, really." She paused as the sound of girlish shrieks reached them from the living room. "Lisa and Jody are back. Come and meet them."

Jody was eleven, her hair cut short in a black cap, her face pixieish, her body still retaining remnants of a baby plumpness. Lisa, who was two years older, had reached the gangly stage of young adolescence and appeared to be all arms and legs, except for the huge dark eyes that dominated her face. *When she fills out,* Rhea thought as they were introduced, *Lisa will be lovely.*

The girls, while they were studiously polite, seemed only mildly curious about Rhea. Their attention was all for their uncle, who kissed and hugged them, then pulled them down beside him on the couch to answer a barage of questions. What had he been doing since Christmas? Why hadn't he written more often? Why couldn't he stay longer than two days? When was he going to let them come to New York for a visit?

Rhea's fears that she might be perceived as an intruder into the family circle were quickly dissipated. She sat in the Bouchers' living room, listening to Thorne and his family catching up on each other and, although she could contribute little to the conversation, she did not feel at all excluded. This was mainly due to Grace, who frequently turned to her with with an offhand remark.

"I wish you could have been with us last Christmas, Rhea," Grace said at one point. "Thorne arrived on our doorstep with the biggest tree you've ever seen—and we'd already decorated a tree. Nothing would do, though, but that we decorate his, as well. So we had a tree in the living room and another in the den."

"It was the best Christmas we ever had," said Lisa emphatically.

"We didn't have enough decorations for two trees," put in Jody, "so we strung popcorn and made cookie ornaments. Uncle Thorne's tree turned out prettier than the other one, didn't it, Mother?"

Later, Grace and Rhea retired to the kitchen to prepare dinner. "You have a wonderful family," Rhea said as she arranged ironstone pottery and silver on the big oak table that sat in one corner of the large country-style kitchen. "I don't know when I've enjoyed myself so much. I'm glad I came."

Grace was turning crisp fried chicken in a big iron skillet on the range. "I'm glad, too, Rhea. You seem to fit into our family perfectly."

In spite of her earlier disclaimer, Rhea realized that Grace wanted to believe there was more between her and Thorne than friendship. She did not bother to set Grace straight again concerning her relationship with Thorne, for she sensed it would probably do no good. Grace obviously wanted to believe that her brother was thinking of settling down, and who would better fit an older sister's conception of a proper mate for Thorne than a Choctaw girl who had grown up only a few miles from Poteau?

After dinner they played cards. Lisa and Jody taught them the game of hearts, and then proceeded, with undisguised relish, to win every hand. There was a great deal of laughter around the big oak table. It was getting quite late when Grace served coffee and the chocolate cake they had been too full to eat with dinner.

As soon as the last bite of her cake was gone, Jody, who

had won the last three hands of hearts, exclaimed, "Let's play one more game."

This was met by a chorus of groans. "You are the most obnoxious winner I've ever met," Thorne told her, rumpling her black hair.

"I think she cheated that last hand," Lisa said.

Jody was highly indignant. "I did not! You're just mad 'cause I won more hands than you did!"

"Stop squabbling, you two." Harold's quiet voice broke into what was showing signs of becoming a heated argument.

"No more tonight, Jody," Grace added. "It's past your bedtime. It's off to dreamland for both of you. Now, scoot!"

"Oh, do we have to?" Jody whined.

"You have to," her father informed her, and there were no further arguments.

Grace went along to help Lisa move the clothes she would need from her room to Jody's. Then Harold stretched and pushed his chair back from the table. "I'm going to hit the hay. See you two in the morning."

Thorne helped Rhea carry the dessert plates and coffee cups to the sink. She washed them while he dried. The dishes done, she turned from the sink to find his head lowered, his face only inches from her own. She felt breathless. "I—I'm ready for bed, too, aren't you?"

His lips, very close to her own murmured, "What man could resist an invitation like that?"

"I didn't mean—oh!" She knew that he was teasing her; nevertheless, she felt hot all over with embarrassment.

Her protests were smothered by his mouth, which descended and touched her own in what began as a light kiss. But suddenly he sighed longingly and his arms crushed her against the hard length of his body, and his kiss became hungry and demanding. She was not capable of stifling an eager response.

How wonderfully male he smells, she thought dreamily, as her arms slid up and around his neck. His mouth tasted faintly and deliciously of chocolate, and his thick hair, as she slipped her fingers through it, felt like heavy sensuous layers of black velvet. Uttering a softly muffled moan, she felt the softness of her body molding itself to the hard muscles of his chest and thighs, felt, too, her body's melting welcome to the thrusting demand of his.

A few moments longer locked in his arms, tasting his greedy kiss, feeling his rising passion, and she would have agreed to anything he asked of her. But she heard Grace's voice in the hall bidding good night to her daughters and was brought to her senses.

Pulling away from him, she whispered, "Your sister is coming. Please let me go."

For a moment, his arms clamped her even more tightly against him, and then his hands came up slowly to frame her face. His dark eyes held a strange, moody look as they caressed her mouth, then moved up to meet her bemused gaze.

"Rhea, I . . ."

Hearing Grace's footsteps coming closer, Rhea pushed gently against his chest.

"Thorne, please. If she finds us like this, we'll all be embarrassed."

With an impatient grunt, he dropped his arms and stepped back. "I hope you're going to be thinking of me tossing in my lonely bed in the den. I'm sure as hell going to be thinking of you."

She slipped past him and started across the kitchen just as Grace appeared in the doorway.

"I'm going to make up the couch in the den for you

now, Thorne," Grace said. "Oh, you didn't need to do those dishes, Rhea."

"It only took a minute," Rhea said, striving to hide her breathlessness and keep her voice steady. "Thorne helped me."

Grace's glance moved from Rhea to her brother, who lounged against the cabinet. There was both curiosity and speculation in that look.

"Good night, Grace." Rhea moved to the door. "I'm going to bed now. Night, Thorne," she said over her shoulder as she passed Grace, praying the other woman couldn't hear the erratic thumping of her heart, and made her way along the hall to the bedroom at the end.

In bed, staring out the window at the star-studded night sky, Rhea pressed fingers against lips that still felt warm and glowing from Thorne's kiss. Before today she had formed a picture of him as an attractive but arrogantly aggressive man whose desires and actions were calculated and basically selfish. Now she had seen him in the bosom of his family, and his affection for his sister and her family was clearly unfeigned and certainly not self-serving. He had been so wonderful with Lisa and Jody, so full of loving warmth. If he could be that good with his nieces, what would he be like with children of his own?

Rhea shivered as her mind dwelt on thoughts of Thorne as an adoring, passionate husband. But the lovely vision was abruptly punctured as Diane Lowery's beautiful face intruded. It seemed more than conceivable that should Thorne ever decide to marry he would choose someone like Diane. Not someone *like* her, Rhea told herself sternly, but Diane, in fact. The woman clearly felt more for him than the agent-client relationship warranted. And Thorne seemed to admire Diane and did not find her sometimes possessive attitude toward him rankling. They needed each other in the business area of their lives. Did they need each other equally as much in other areas?

Pure jealousy spread through Rhea, twisting painfully in the pit of her stomach and clumping up in her chest. She pressed her eyelids closed and a tear slid down one cheek. She actually had to push her clenched fist against her mouth to stifle a moan of desperation.

I am behaving like a total fool, her mind berated her fiercely. *This crazy infatuation with Thorne will pass, as all infatuations must. And infatuation is all it is. Such an excruciatingly painful feeling cannot be love. Besides, I cannot be in love with a man I've known only two weeks. Anyone with a shred of common sense would know that he is not the right man for me, and I am certainly not the right woman for him. Furthermore, if these bewildering emotions he arouses in me had anything to do with love, I would put his best interests ahead of my own, acknowledge our unsuitability, and hope he finds happiness with Diane or someone like her.*

She did not hope that at all, however. She couldn't stand the thought of Thorne's loving another woman. She could only acknowledge her own desperate need to be the recipient of all his loving impulses. To be absolutely honest, she wished with all her being that she was at that very moment in Thorne's arms again.

At least she had acknowledged the pitiful weakness in herself. Now she had only to get through the rest of the weekend with some semblance of composure.

This resolution proved easier made than accomplished. After sleeping late the next morning, the family met in the kitchen for a hearty brunch. The meal finished, the men and the two young girls stretched out on the carpeted floor in the living room to watch a professional boxing match on television. After cleaning the kitchen, Grace and Rhea joined them.

Sitting in a comfortable overstuffed chair in the corner, Rhea let her glance take in Thorne's long, lean body flanked by his two nieces. He wore faded jeans that rode low on his hips and clung to his muscled legs like a second skin. His shirt was a yellow ribbed knit with a slashed V opening in front that exposed deeply tanned skin stretched over hard chest muscles. He looked like a powerful jungle beast in repose, and Rhea felt a warm tingling along her nerve ends as her eyes took in the well-developed masculine outlines of his body.

As she watched, he stirred and sat up. He threw an arm around each of his nieces and hugged them against his sides, his eyes traveling to meet Rhea's lingering look. She glanced away from him, flushing as if she'd been caught in some indecent act.

"I hate to say it, but we've got to get started back to the city," Thorne said, giving the girls a final squeeze.

Naturally this announcement was met by impassioned pleas from Lisa and Jody to stay just a little while longer. Thorne got to his feet in one lithe movement and stood, grinning down at the girls. "No can do, younguns. Rhea has to work tomorrow, and I have to go to Texas."

Actually Rhea had not expected they would be leaving quite so early herself—it was only one o'clock. She even discovered a reluctance to separate from the Bouchers. They were such a warm, happy family, and they had made her feel like one of them.

Nevertheless, she took her cue from Thorne and went to the bedroom to collect her overnight case. She was wearing denim shorts and a red cotton shirt with backless leather sandals, and she decided the outfit would be more comfortable for the long drive—and more in keeping with

Thorne's casual attire—than the only other change of clothes she had brought, a lightweight silk dress.

When she returned to the living room, Thorne had his suitcase ready, and after hugs and good-byes all around, they took their leave. It was a hot, bright summer day, the sort of day that makes one appreciate air-conditioned automobiles. Rhea relaxed against the plush upholstery of the rented car while Thorne fiddled with the radio until he found an FM station that played soft, relaxing music.

When they turned onto the highway, Rhea sat forward in her seat with sudden alertness. "Why did you turn south? Oklahoma City is in the opposite direction."

"We're not going to Oklahoma City—just yet," Thorne informed her calmly.

"We're not? But where *are* we going?"

"Don't panic," he drawled, giving her an amused look. "We're going for a little drive in the country. Didn't you say your grandfather once lived in the woods near here?"

"Yes, but he sold the cabin before he died. Strangers will be living there now—if it's still fit for human habitation."

"If someone's living there, we won't bother them. But I thought you'd like to see it again." He glanced over at her. "I wasn't wrong, was I?"

"No, but—" She studied the chiseled angles of his profile for a moment. "Why are you doing this?"

"I told you why," he said with a flat edge to the words. His cool assurance sent a shiver of apprehension up Rhea's backbone. Some feminine instinct warned her to protest, to demand that he turn the car around and head for Oklahoma City without delay. But giving voice to her fears required more courage than she possessed. So she merely slumped back against the seat and remained silent.

After a moment Thorne said easily, "You'll have to tell me where to turn off."

She recognized the road even though several new houses had been built along the highway since last she'd visited the area. And once they'd turned into the woods, it looked so much as she remembered that they might have moved back in time fifteen years. She began to feel a mounting anticipation and pressed close to the side window to look into the deep green of the woods and recall wandering there as a child.

"The cabin should be just around this bend," she said. Remembering her grandfather and those carefree days made her throat feel tight and achy and she swallowed hard, feeling ridiculously close to tears. She pointed suddenly. "There it is. Oh, it looks so small and dilapidated . . ."

Thorne stopped the car on the grassy verge alongside the road. "Looks vacant," he said, opening the door and climbing out. Rhea followed and they walked slowly through the trees toward the cabin, stopping to look up at the sagging front door and boarded-up front windows.

They stepped onto the porch and Thorne pushed at the door with his shoulder until it opened far enough for them to enter. The boards at the front windows cut off most of the sunlight. The interior of the small cabin was dim and dusty. Rhea stood looking about with a feeling of sadness. "I wonder what happened to the furniture?"

"Somebody carted it off, I suppose."

"It wasn't worth anything really," Rhea told him, "but the cabin looks so lonely and sad like this."

He wandered about the room, looking into the cabinets and coming to a stop in front of the massive stone fireplace. "It's not as bad as it looks. It wouldn't take a great deal of money for somebody to fix it up as a summer place."

Rhea took one last look around, then headed for the door. "I'm going outside to see if I can find the treehouse my grandfather made for me when I was eight."

Behind the cabin, the trees grew thicker than she remembered from her childhood, or maybe it only seemed so because she had been so much smaller then and could slip through the tightest places easily. There had been a path leading to the big hackberry where she'd spent so many happy hours in her treehouse, but it had become overgrown and she could find no trace of it.

She made her way cautiously through the trees, letting the silence of the woods enclose her—a silence more profound and serene than any other she had ever known. Then she saw the spreading branches of the hackberry tree ahead with the small grassy clearing beneath it that she remembered. Upon reaching the tree, she ran her hand over the rough, aged bark and peered up into the branches. The boards that her grandfather had nailed to the trunk to be used as a ladder were gone, and she couldn't see any sign of the treehouse either.

Sounds of movement through the fallen leaves and underbrush reached her and she turned as Thorne appeared at the edge of the clearing.

"The look on your face tells me this is a special place to you," he said.

A reflective smile curved her lips. "I spent hours and hours playing here as a child. There's nothing left of my treehouse now, but you're right, this is a special place."

He returned her smile. "Do you allow intruders to enter?"

In her progress through the trees, the combs that held her hair away from her face had come out and she had

70

thrust them into the pocket of her shirt. Under the lazy scrutiny of Thorne's dark eyes she was suddenly made aware of her hair spilling about her face in hopeless disarray. For the first time, too, she realized that her trek through the humid closeness of the woods had caused a film of perspiration to break out on her body, which made her red shirt and denim shorts cling to her in a way that left little to the imagination. She was convinced that no single item of her state of dishevelment had escaped his notice. The dark eyes were all-encompassing, and she tugged at the clinging dampness of her shirt in a futile effort to hide the soft fullness of her breasts from him.

"Of course, you may come in," she said foolishly, responding belatedly to his teasing question and realizing, as she did so, that his unexpected appearance, when memories of her childhood had made her feel raw and vulnerable, had temporarily stripped her of the composed facade she had vowed to wear until they parted.

He ambled across the grassy floor of the clearing and stopped a few feet from her, supporting himself with one hand against the hackberry's trunk. His posture spread the V of his shirt to reveal the strong outlines of his chest. "You look about eight years old again," he remarked, as his eyes roamed familiarly over the length of her body, and then he added with an ironic smile, "Well, almost."

Vainly she tried again to push her hair into some semblance of order. "I'm sure I must look a mess," she ventured at last, choosing her words carefully.

"I didn't mean that at all," he exclaimed, pushing himself away from the tree and moving closer to her. "You look charmingly . . . tousled." He was only inches from her now, so close that she could actually feel the heat emanating from his body and it made her feel far too defenseless and weak. She considered walking away from him, far enough to put a safe distance between them; but such an action somehow seemed undignified, and besides, it would confirm what she was certain he already suspected, that he made her feel unsure of herself.

"I think we'd better go, Thorne," she said tremulously, endeavoring not to look as anxious as she felt. "It—it was kind of you to bring me here, and—"

"It wasn't kind at all," he interrupted. "I wanted to be alone with you someplace where I wasn't occupied with driving. Rhea, I've enjoyed this weekend more than anything I can remember in a very long time." He reached out a hand to touch her cheek.

"It was nice that you could be with your sister and her family—"

"That was part of it, yes." The words were edged with something she couldn't fathom. "But partly it was because you were there. I got the feeling that you were enjoying it, too."

His fingers slowly traced the outline of her jaw and chin, and Rhea's instinctive flinching away from his touch brought a sharp look of irritation to his eyes. "There is no need for you to be afraid of me," he told her, looking down at her with a faint scowl. Her gaze took in the firm, tan texture of his facial skin, and the strong column of his throat rising from the yellow V of his shirt. The clean odor of his body mingled with the citrus aroma of his shaving lotion assailed her nostrils. His black hair lay smoothly across his forehead and shaped itself to his head, shining and clean without any trace of dressing or spray. She saw a pulse beating at the base of his throat. Her eyes clung to that quickening pulsebeat for a long moment before she looked up again swiftly.

"Thorne—"

She put out a hand to ward him off, but he was immovable. Her fingers made contact with the hard bareness of his chest, and as she jerked them away in confusion, his fingers lifted her hair to expose her ear and he bent his head and lightly touched the lobe with his lips.

It was an almost tentative caress, but Rhea trembled as a fusion of sensations rippled through her. Slowly his arm encircled her waist and her body was brought close against his.

"Thorne—" she uttered again, even more weakly than before, but the smoldering passion of his gaze paralyzed her tongue. She stared up at him, her lips parted, struck dumb. And when he bent his head again, almost involuntarily her mouth lifted to meet his. The experience was as overwhelming as his previous kisses had been—if possible, more so. A dizzying surge of hot blood rushed to her head and quickly spread through her body as the pressure of his embrace increased.

Her fingers worked spasmodically at the fabric of his shirt in a blind attempt to get some control over her careening senses. Then she was crushed against him, his hands moving down to the curve of her hips to haul her against the powerful muscles of his thighs.

"You feel so good, Rhea . . ."

The words were spoken against her mouth, and a profound sense of helplessness gripped her. He knew exactly how to arouse a woman, and she was no match for the slow, measured skill with which he brought her with him along the path of rising sensual desire. At no point was there a need to overcome her protests, for she uttered not a one. By the time she became keenly aware of the pulsing need of his body, she had no other wish than to answer that need with her own inflamed response. The only sounds she made then were incoherent pleas for release, not from the demand of his embrace, but from the clamoring hunger of her own body.

And by the time his hand moved unhurriedly to free her of her clothing, she was too caught up in the new wonder of the experience to be fully aware of what he was doing or to care very much. It was only when his mouth began exploring the secret places of her body that she was jolted into full awareness of her utter exposure to him.

"Oh, Thorne . . . we can't . . ." she gasped out, but there was no conviction in the words and he did not heed them. Instead, he lifted her breast in one hand and began to stroke the swelling tip with the fingers of his other hand.

"Last night, all alone in my bed, I imagined doing this," he said, his voice low and thick with feeling. "You are even more beautiful than I dreamed." He bent his head and enclosed the taut nipple with his lips.

She gasped at the sharp thrill that passed through her body as he explored it more intimately than any man had ever done before.

She whispered his name and he lifted her in his arms. Her sandals slipped from her dangling feet and fell to the ground as he carried her to a spot where the grass was thick and soft and springy. There he lay her down and, with a few deft movements, shed his clothes, then knelt beside her, his gaze traveling over her with smoldering fire in its depths. The intensity of his regard made her hot with sudden embarrassment. She closed her eyes and her arms came up to cover her breasts. He caught her hands and lifted them gently above her head. "Don't ever be ashamed of your body. I have never seen anything so beautiful. Look at me, Rhea."

She opened her eyes and, totally bemused, let her senses take in the beautiful, lean strength of him—the broad shoulders and hard chest, the flat stomach and lean hips, and the bold evidence of his desire.

"I—I don't know if I can—I've never—" she got out chokingly.

"I knew that the first time I saw you," he said huskily, slowly lowering his body to lie beside her. "Don't you remember? But there is nothing to fear, Rhea. I won't hurt you. I'll stop any time you want me to."

Rhea was trembling with longings she had never known before and, hardly aware of what she was doing, she let her hand trace a tentative exploration across his rib cage and over the jutting bone of his hip. "You—will?"

"Yes." He bent to nibble her shoulder with his lips. "Umm—you taste delicious."

She sighed and, giving in to a fierce desire to touch his body, to explore its mysteries, she ran her hands across his shoulders and back caressingly, causing him to moan deep in his throat. Thrusting aside her last lingering doubts, she wound her arms around his neck and pressed his mouth down to her with hungry urgency.

Suddenly she could not get close enough to him, and instinctively she moved beneath him, arching her body against the whole hard length of him, her body yearning to know more and more of his. The smooth ripple of his back muscles, warm and moist and male, spread beneath her palms. Her fingers learned more intimately the outlines of his shoulders, traced the shape of his ears and the hard muscles of his neck, then moved lower to his waist and lean hips. She wanted to memorize his body, to know it better than she knew her own, and she lost herself in the delight of the learning.

Thorne's mouth ravaged hers as his hands conducted their own exploration until she was totally submissive and yielding in his arms. He lifted his head and looked at her

75

with passion-glazed eyes. "Rhea," he whispered hoarsely, "tell me now if you want me to stop."

Her answer was a moan of surrender as her lips sought once more the ravenous demand of his. What followed was as inevitable as the changing of the seasons, as beautifully natural as the lush, green woods and the mottled sunlight falling through the boughed ceiling across their bodies and the grassy floor of the bower where they lay.

So lost in the incomprehensible wonder of what was happening, Rhea was hardly aware of the single, brief stab of pain as she gave herself up to the devouring need of his kiss and the movement of his body. At the moment when she thought she could not bear anymore sensuous pleasure, something began to build inside her—a warm, tingling pressure that made her feel as if she were rushing for the edge of a cliff. And suddenly she plunged with Thorne over the edge of physical fulfillment into ecstasy that she wanted never to end.

Slowly, driftingly, she sank back to earth and time. Her whole body sated and moistly glowing, she looked into Thorne's bemused face and knew that she had given more than her body. She had given her heart and her soul to this man and she reveled in his slow, gentle kiss that expressed far better than words the wonder of what they had shared.

Chapter 4

Rhea's body trembled now as she turned away from the night pressing against the cabin window and let the curtain fall into place. She moved back to the fireplace and placed another log on the fire, striving to drive out the images that threatened to destroy the comforting solitude of her cabin retreat.

Thorne's lovemaking had shown her a world of powerful emotions that she had not even known existed. It was just her bad luck that no other man had ever aroused her as Thorne had been able to do with a touch or a mere look. There had been no one else for Rhea after Thorne, but she was certain there had been other women for him. And before, during, and after there had been Diane Lowery.

Even now the pain of that betrayal pierced her like a stiletto. And with the pain, the images returned. She sank into one of the corduroy chairs and let them come, resigned to reliving all of it one last time. Perhaps it would serve as a catharsis, and afterward she could exorcise that part of her past forever from her memory.

She remembered how horrified she had been when her brain dispelled the fog caused by their lovemaking and rational thought returned. She could not believe that she had given herself so easily, that a single brief encounter could so disrupt the standards that had always been important to her. She was utterly shaken by what Thorne had enkindled in her. She wanted only to bolt, to find some other way to return home. Instead, she had to endure the long drive to Oklahoma City with Thorne, who did nothing to make the enforced physical closeness easier for her to bear.

During much of the drive he brooded silently, leaving her to her own devices, which, under the circumstances, were nonexistent. When he did speak, it was of impersonal things. *The most shattering experience of my life,* she told herself, *meant no more to him than stopping for a quick hamburger!*

Consequently she was totally unprepared for the grim announcement he made when he deposited her at her front door. "We'll get married right away," he said in a cool but decisive tone.

She was at first convinced that she could not have heard him correctly. But, as she stared at the stubborn line of his jaw, she realized she had, and she laughed, a reaction caused not by amusement, but near hysteria.

"Must you make this even more difficult for me," she demanded in a shrill voice, "by treating the whole thing as some kind of practical joke?"

"I'm perfectly serious," he told her, a sharp edge of anger making the words brittle. No inquiries as to how she felt about the matter, no professions of love. At least he wasn't going to be *that* hypocritical!

"Stop talking nonsense, Thorne," she said flatly. "You're just feeling guilty about taking advantage of me."

His jaw hardened even more as she watched. "You're not being fair, Rhea. But I admit I am feeling a little guilty. That's not the only—"

"Stop it!" she cut him off, clenching her hands into fists to keep from slapping him. "People do not get married after two weeks' acquaintance. You've made your noble gesture, Thorne, so will you please go? You will thank me in the morning. In fact, you probably already are." She whirled about and fumbled her apartment key into the lock, turning it viciously.

"You know where I'll be if you change your mind," he said. She thought she detected a hint of relief in the icy accents and, without replying, stepped inside her apartment and slammed the door in his face.

The next few days were the most depressing she could ever remember. Again and again she relived what had happened, each time reaffirming her conviction that she was nothing but another compliant female body to Thorne. It was not possible, she thought, to feel more used and humiliated than she did. On that score she was wrong, as she discovered when Diane Lowery telephoned her on Wednesday night of the week following her weekend with Thorne.

"Rhea," said Diane, "I know you'll think this is none of my business, but I like you—I really do—and I couldn't live with myself if I didn't try to warn you."

"Warn me?" Rhea hadn't the faintest idea what the woman was getting at.

"May I speak frankly?"

"I wish you would."

"Thorne told me about your weekend together."

Her words went through Rhea like jagged shards of glass. She had known that the weekend had been merely another "fling" in a long line of them for Thorne. In fact,

79

hadn't he told her at their first meeting that that was what he had in mind? But to tell Diane what had happened! They had probably laughed about Rhea's stupidity over drinks! It was the final humiliation.

"He—he had no right to do that." The words fell quiveringly from stiff lips.

"I know," agreed Diane sympathetically. "Aren't men the pits? But don't be too angry with him. You know how men love to brag about their little conquests."

"I'm—finding out," Rhea stammered, almost choking on her anger.

"Look, Rhea, Thorne and I have been together for a long time. I'm sure you've suspected that we're lovers, so I'm not telling you anything you aren't already aware of. And this isn't the first time Thorne has strayed. I've learned to handle his little . . . indiscretions. Thorne and I understand each other, which is why he always comes back to me. There is a strong bond between us, but at the same time we give each other breathing space. Usually, when he feels he has to prove his independence by seducing another woman, I figure she can take care of herself. But I know you aren't accustomed to sleeping around and—"

Rhea had remained silent as long as she could. "How dare you!" she exploded.

"Please, let me finish," Diane went on as calmly as if Rhea had not spoken. "I said I know you're an old-fashioned sort of girl. It sticks out all over you, dear, and I don't mean that as an insult, either. That's why I felt I had to warn you not to pin any hopes on Thorne. I know better than anyone how persuasive he is when he wants to be. Just don't take too seriously anything he might have said in, shall we say, a vulnerable moment?"

Rhea forestalled any more of the woman's audacious

admonitions by slamming down the receiver. Diane Lowery was as hard and unfeeling as Thorne. My God, what kind of people lived like that? She hated them—both of them!

Gradually, over the next few weeks, the hurt, lost feeling that was Thorne's legacy to Rhea began to dull. She kept very busy with friends in the evenings and on weekends, dating two young men whom she had known in college. She told herself that Thorne Folsom was merely an unfortunate interlude in her life, and the sooner she forgot him and everything connected with him, the better. She had begun to believe that time really would heal her wounds.

And then one evening in mid-September she stepped out of a shower to hear a knock at her door. Quickly she wrapped a terry robe around herself and went to the door to find Thorne standing on the front step.

"Hello, Rhea."

Every detail was just as she remembered—the tall, athletic body in corduroy jeans and a light sweater, the craggy face with the deep brown eyes and shining black hair, the same crooked half smile. And all the feelings—the dizzying weakness, the swelling in her chest, the tightening of her throat—that she thought she was beginning to put behind her were just as strong as ever.

When she found her voice, it sounded hoarse and far away. "What—what are you doing here?"

"May I come in?" Without waiting for a reply, he walked past her into the living room. He stood in front of the sofa, shoulders hunched slightly, hands thrust into the pockets of his jeans. His eyes swept from her black hair, pinned loosely atop her head but escaping down her neck in damp strands, to her bare feet, and he grinned appreciatively. "Were you getting ready to go out?"

She was not, but she had no intention of telling him so. "I asked you a question. What are you doing here?"

"Aren't you even going to ask me to sit down?"

Impatience sharpened her tongue. "Why bother? I'm sure you will, anyway."

One eyebrow lifted challengingly, but he remained standing. "You don't mean to make this easy for me, do you? Okay, Rhea, we'll do it your way." He took a step toward her, and she jumped back as if she'd been burned. She put a chair between them and stood gripping its back with whitened fingers.

For a moment she saw something hurt and vulnerable in his dark eyes, but this only stiffened her resolve to keep her distance.

"I've thought about you every waking minute since I left here," he said quietly.

"Really?" she inquired flippantly. "I suppose I should have suspected that from all those phone calls and letters." Her sarcasm was so thick it almost choked her.

"I didn't call or write because I wasn't sure you wanted to hear from me," he said simply.

"Very astute of you! So why are you here now?"

"Because I couldn't stay away any longer." The words hung in the air between them as they stared at each other. Rhea did not trust herself to move, and she sensed that Thorne was exerting a great strength of will to remain where he was. He ran a hand through his thick hair in a gesture of mingled impatience and frustration. "I haven't been able to work. I don't sleep well. When you turned down my proposal, I swore I'd forget you. I find that I can't." He paused, then took a long breath. "I love you, Rhea. I want you, I need you. I'm here to ask you again—to plead with you—to marry me."

"Wh-what?" The whispered question was barely audible in the silent room. She was too confused to think clearly. Could Thorne actually be standing there telling her that he loved her, that he wanted and needed her? After all that had happened, she could not believe he was sincere. But what could he hope to gain by saying these things?

"You heard me, Rhea," he said quietly. "I know I deserve it, but do you really mean to go on punishing me?"

If he really cared for her, would he have told Diane what had happened between them? "What about Diane?"

"Diane?" He looked nonplussed, and then he ducked his head briefly before meeting her gaze again. "I won't lie to you, Rhea. Diane and I were . . . intimate for a short time, but that part of our relationship had ended before I ever met you. I never loved her—or anyone else until you. But I can't stand here and tell you there haven't been other women in my life. If you can't live with that, maybe you *should* turn me down—except I won't let you." He sounded so earnest, but Diane's words echoed in her memory: *Thorne and I understand each other, which is why he always comes back to me.*

"Diane called me after you went to Texas. She said you told her what happened between us that weekend we went to Poteau."

"She said—?" He was very thoughtful for a moment. "She kept asking me what had put me into such a black mood. Finally, I told her you went with me that weekend and that we'd had a disagreement." His eyes narrowed. "Diane's shrewd. Evidently she drew her own conclusions from what I said."

You know how men love to brag about their little conquests. No, no, it wasn't true, it couldn't be! Rhea was caught in the trap of her own emotions. She was a fool even to consider his proposal, she thought wildly, but the

83

trouble was she couldn't bear the thought of seeing him walk out of her life again, either.

"Rhea, Rhea . . ." he murmured with such husky pleading that it tore at her heart. He came to her side and, capturing her cold hands, he lifted them to his lips and kissed her palms with bone-melting intimacy. "I love you, my darling. Please believe that."

Her protests died before they reached her lips, and her resistance crumbled in the face of the naked need she saw in his eyes. She believed him because she wanted so desperately to do so. Uncaring of the consequences, wanting to feel his arms around her, to belong to him utterly, she flung herself against his broad chest. Tears of relief and happiness coursed down her cheeks. "Oh, Thorne, hold me . . . please, please, just hold me . . ."

They were married three days later in the Boucher's living room in Poteau. They spent two nights in a rustic log cabin in the Ouachita National Forest before leaving for New York. The hectic hustle of a city of that size was totally alien to Rhea and, in fact, intimidating. The roar of traffic, the jostling pedestrians in the crowded streets assaulted her senses harshly. But she vowed to learn to live in Thorne's world because she wanted, in all things, to please him.

They moved into a luxurious apartment that came with daily maid service. Rhea insisted upon doing all the cooking, however, and she certainly had plenty of time in which to try out gourmet recipes while Thorne worked in his study in the apartment.

The apartment became her safe, serene little world, and forays into the noisy streets became less unpleasant because the apartment was always there waiting for her return. The only real flaw in an otherwise idyllic existence,

84

as far as Rhea was concerned, was the fact that Diane Lowery, as Thorne's agent, was frequently in his company. Negotiations were underway with the film company for Thorne to write the screenplay that was to be made from his second novel. Thorne's earlier objections had been overcome by a great deal of money and the promise of an experienced script writer as collaborator. Settling all the details of the agreement required numerous phone calls and meetings between Thorne and Diane, and Rhea was still unsure enough of her place in Thorne's affection that she suffered pangs of jealousy whenever she knew the two were together.

Even so, those early weeks were heavenly. Thorne was everything she had ever dreamed of in a lover, and Rhea was certain no woman had ever been as happy and content as she. The knowledge that she was living in a fool's paradise did not break upon her until they had been married for three months. It began one evening after Thorne received a telephone call from Diane.

Rhea was in the kitchen trying out a new recipe for a Cornish hen baked in wine sauce. Thorne came into the room and, as she turned from the stove, caught her up in his arms and kissed her tenderly.

"Ummm," he said after a moment. "Something smells delicious."

"It's your dinner."

He frowned. "Do you think it'll keep until tomorrow, sweetheart? I have to go out for dinner tonight. There's a meeting with the film company's representatives."

Rhea moved out of his arms. "And Diane, of course."

"Of course." He looked at her in some perplexity. "Diane *is* my agent. You know she handles my business affairs."

"Why doesn't she handle them then?" Rhea inquired,

unable, for once, to hide her dislike and jealousy of the beautiful brunette. "Why do you have to be in on all these meetings?"

His sigh was heavy with exasperation. "Because I'm the one most directly involved."

"What about me?" Her voice had become shrill but she was too disappointed at the prospect of spending another evening alone to care. "After all, I'm certainly going to be involved if you have to move to California. But I'm never invited to these meetings Diane sets up."

She could see that Thorne was becoming angry. "It never occurred to Diane or me that you would have the slightest interest in sitting through a discussion of percentages and options and subsidiary rights. You don't know anything about those things, and you'd be bored stiff after the first five minutes."

The condescension she thought she heard in his tone made her lose her already skimpy hold on her composure. "So what else is new? I get bored sitting around here night after night while you go out galavanting with Diane Lowery!"

"Rhea," he said sternly, "you're behaving like a spoiled child." He glanced distractedly at his watch. "I haven't time to deal with your insecurities right now. I have to shower and dress. We'll discuss this when I get back if you insist, although I hope by then you will have seen that you're making a mountain out of a molehill."

He turned on his heel and walked out of the kitchen, leaving her shaking with anger and resentment. She put the meal in the refrigerator and shut herself into the spare bedroom until she heard Thorne leaving the apartment, and any hope she might have nursed that he would apologize for his harsh words was gone.

She roamed restlessly through the shadowy apartment,

trying not to imagine Thorne and Diane together, yet unable to stop her thoughts from going over what Diane had said to her in that telephone call before she and Thorne were married. Was it true that Thorne always returned to Diane's arms? Would he do such a thing even after exchanging wedding vows with Rhea? Recalling the note of assurance that had rung in Diane's voice during that conversation, Rhea shivered as if she were in the grip of a fever.

Her mind told her that Thorne could not avoid spending some time with Diane as long as she was his agent, but her emotions balked at the thought. There were dozens of agents in New York. Why did Thorne stubbornly refuse to consider switching to one of them if, indeed, his relationship with Diane was merely business? Oh, she knew all the arguments he could give. Diane had believed in his work when he was still a struggling, unpublished writer. She had given him the encouragement to continue writing when he felt it was useless to go on. She had persisted until she found a publisher for him and then had gotten uncharacteristically generous contract terms for a first novelist. Diane Lowery was making him a wealthy man. It never seemed to occur to Thorne that Diane's commissions from his earnings were helping her become one of the most prosperous agents in the country. When Rhea had pointed that out to him, he had said, "I don't begrudge her a dime. She's earned it."

For the hundredth time Rhea told herself she must learn to live with Thorne's loyalty to Diane. After all, he had chosen to marry Rhea. And Diane had accepted the state of affairs with apparent equanimity. She was civil to Rhea when they met, although Rhea took pains never to be alone with the other woman.

After an hour spent thus reasoning with herself, Rhea

was calm enough to fix her dinner, an omelet and hot, spiced tea, which she had on a tray in front of the television set. As soon as Thorne returned, they must sit down and discuss her feelings calmly, she told herself. Nothing could be solved by hiding her anxieties and uncertainties from her husband.

If Thorne had come home at a reasonable hour, they might have reached a better understanding of each other. But as midnight came and went and then one o'clock, all of Rhea's hurt and frustration returned. Was he staying away deliberately, to punish her? The more she considered it, the angrier she became. By one thirty, she wanted nothing so much as to hurt him as he was hurting her. In a fit of rebellious frustration she phoned for a taxi and went to an all-night movie house not far from the apartment building. She imagined Thorne coming home in the middle of the night to find her gone. He would be beside himself with worry. The thought gave her a grim satisfaction. Let him discover what it felt like.

Her righteous indignation carried her through one film, although she couldn't have said afterward what the story concerned. But as the credits for the second film flashed upon the screen, she began to doubt the wisdom of quitting the apartment without even leaving a note telling Thorne where she had gone. It was true that Thorne's insensitive response to her outburst earlier had hurt her, but she didn't think it was deliberate. What she was doing was a calculated attempt to punish. Further, she knew Thorne well enough by now to realize that such immature striking back would only make matters worse.

Assailed by a growing feeling of impending disaster, she gathered up her handbag and coat and left the theater quickly. She waited in the lobby for a half hour, berating herself for behaving like the spoiled child Thorne had accused her of being, before the taxi she had summoned arrived.

Back at the apartment, she felt weak with relief when she saw Thorne's topcoat thrown across a living room chair. A table lamp had been left on.

"Thorne?"

Receiving no reply, she hung her coat in the entry closet and hurried along the carpeted hallway toward the master bedroom. Surely he could not have gone to sleep after finding her gone. He would be angry with her for leaving the apartment as she had, but she would beg for his forgiveness, if necessary. She wanted only to be reassured by the feel of Thorne's warm body pressed against her own.

Just as she reached the closed bedroom door, it opened. Diane Lowery, carrying her coat and shoes in one hand and trying to button her blouse with the other, stepped out.

Rhea went cold and then hot all over. The two women stood stock-still for a moment, staring at each other. A strange prickle of pure hatred made the hair on the back of Rhea's neck rise.

"What are you doing here?" she demanded in a low, shaking voice.

Diane gave up trying to fasten her blouse and shrugged into her coat. Her beautiful classic features were flushed with embarrassment or triumph—Rhea couldn't tell which.

In the dim hallway Diane's golden cat's eyes glittered like chips of amber. She swayed slightly as she bent to put on her shoes. Straightening, she said, "I wouldn't have had you walk in here like this for anything in the world, Rhea. He told me you'd gone back to Oklahoma for a visit."

Rhea's dark eyes flashed, brilliant with pain and anger.

"I don't believe you." Finding her gone, he *must* have been worried. He could not have dismissed her so carelessly.

"Don't then, if it makes this any easier for you," Diane said in a tone of reasonableness that made Rhea want to claw her beautiful face. "I did try to warn you about Thorne," she went on calmly. "Poor, gullible Rhea. Well, whether you believe me or not, I wouldn't have stayed if I'd known you were in town. Thorne had a lot to drink tonight. Perhaps he wasn't thinking clearly—" The malicious note was unmistakable now.

Rhea stood frozen, despairingly shaking her head. The last bit of warm blood left her face and she was trembling all over. "Get out," she whispered, shivering.

Darting a quick look over her shoulder at the darkened bedroom, Diane said in a contemptuous tone, "This was bound to happen sooner or later, Rhea. This marriage is smothering Thorne. Isn't it time you grew up and accepted that?" Flinging her tousled brown hair away from her face with a toss of her head, she walked away from Rhea. A moment later the sound of a door opening and closing echoed in the quiet apartment.

Rhea bent her head, weak, trembling, so sick she felt she might pass out if she didn't get hold of herself. As soon as she could control her movements, she walked into the bedroom. In the shaft of pale light from the hallway, Thorne lay sprawled on his stomach across the bed in nothing but his jockey shorts. As she came closer to the bed, the smell of the whiskey he had drunk assailed her quivering nostrils. The alcohol combined with Diane's presence had probably prevented his even noticing that Rhea was gone!

His dark, angular face was turned toward her, the slow measured breaths of deep sleep escaping his parted lips.

Dead to the world, he hadn't heard the confrontation between her and Diane in the hallway. The next day he might not even remember what had happened between him and Diane, but that didn't make the knowledge any easier for Rhea to bear. She stared down at him, tears running down her face, and after a moment she walked to the window and leaned her forehead against the cold glass.

She could not bear it. The past three months had been a dream come true for her. She had been deliriously happy and fulfilled, and she had been naive enough to believe it was the same for Thorne. Instead, he had been feeling smothered, as Diane had so viciously pointed out. In the span of a few brief moments, Rhea had been changed irrevocably. Moments ago only love had filled her body and her heart and her mind. Now her body trembled with a bone-deep cold that she did not think would ever go away, and her mind and her heart were lost in a quagmire of confused emotions. She knew she would never be the same again.

Her marriage was over. There was not the slightest doubt about that. With hands that shook, she took a suitcase from her closet and crammed as much of her wardrobe into it as she could. She was making no particular effort to be quiet, but there was no sound of movement from the bed. Rhea was aware of this although, after turning away from him, she did not look again at the sleeping form of her husband.

By the time she carried her suitcase into the living room and phoned for a taxi to take her to the airport, a strange numbing detachment had overtaken her. With hands that seemed almost to belong to someone else, she took a sheet of paper and pen from a desk drawer and wrote:

91

I see now that our marriage was a mistake from the beginning. I'm going home. Don't try to contact me.

She left the note lying on the coffee table and, moving stiffly, put on her coat and gloves and went downstairs to the apartment foyer to wait, for the second time that night, for a taxi.

Chapter 5

The first faint gray of dawn had lightened the sky while Rhea relived her past. Night had passed and she hadn't slept a wink. Coming slowly back to the present, she realized that more tears had fallen as she sat huddled on the couch, remembering. She had held her feelings in check for so long that it was inevitable they would have to come out sometime. So she had cried four years' worth of tears for her broken marriage and for the innocent she had been when she met Thorne. But now the tears were behind her. She was finished with the past and all the regrets resulting from it. She would gain strength during her days at the cabin. Then she would be able to face Thorne one final time and agree to a divorce with calmness and dignity.

Thank goodness he had taken her at her word and had not tried to get in touch with her after she left New York —except for that one time. It was about a month after she had returned to Oklahoma City. She had just been released from the hospital and was still in a state of anguish over what she had been through. Thorne's voice on the other end of the telephone line had seemed the final hurt in days of pain.

"I thought you would have called me by now," he said after a terse greeting.

"I said all I had to say in my note," she told him, actually gritting her teeth to keep from sobbing at the sense of desolation that the sound of his voice was only making worse.

"Why couldn't you have stayed long enough to face me and discuss our problems? I don't understand what you want of me, Rhea."

After seeing Diane leaving his bed, Rhea couldn't imagine what good discussing it would have done. Even now she could not mention Diane's name to Thorne. It would accomplish nothing, and she was in no fit state for accusations or recriminations. Too much had happened since she had left Thorne. If she hadn't been sure it was over then, hearing his voice, with the barely controlled anger in it, removed all doubt. She had been right not to tell him about—but, no. If she allowed her thoughts to go over that ground again, she would lose the last shreds of self-control to which she was clinging so precariously.

"Talking wouldn't have helped," she said finally in low tones. "The fact that you can say you don't understand what I want only proves it."

After a long pause, he asked abruptly, "Do you want a divorce?"

She ran a shaking hand over cheeks that felt cold and clammy. "Whatever you want, Thorne," she said wearily.

"We're discussing what you want," he said in clipped accents. "*You* left *me,* remember?"

Her teeth bit into her lip so hard that she tasted the salty tang of her own blood. "I—I'm not feeling well just now. Couldn't we talk about this at another time?"

"What is it? Are you ill?" If she hadn't known better, she might have believed she heard concern in the sharp questions.

"It's—only a head cold," she lied.

"You'll be needing money," he said finally. "Until we've reached some sort of agreement, I'll send you a monthly check."

"No!" The last thing she needed was charity from Thorne. "I have my old job back at the historical society. I don't need anything more."

He made a harsh, bitter sound. "I see. Your old job and Don Cragmont's broad shoulder to cry on. Right?"

She sighed helplessly. "That doesn't even deserve an answer, Thorne." She drew a long breath. "We can't even speak on the telephone without fighting, can we? I—I have to go now."

"Good-bye, Rhea." There was a sharp click as the connection was severed.

The conversation had ended on such a note of finality that Rhea had expected to be served with divorce papers shortly. As time passed and she began to realize that it wasn't going to happen, she put the last conversation with Thorne out of her mind along with that sorrowful period in her life of which it had seemed the culmination.

Now, after all this time, Thorne had come back to Oklahoma. Rhea got up from the couch and went into the bedroom to get dressed. It had taken four years, she mused as she put on jeans with a cream-colored cowl-necked sweater, but when she returned to the city in a week or so, she would at last be strong enough to face him.

She brushed her hair vigorously, then pulled it back at the temples, securing it with combs. After brushing her teeth, she scrubbed her face and applied moisturizing cream and lip gloss. She piled more logs on the fire before going into the kitchen to prepare breakfast.

She popped biscuits from a can into the oven, then made coffee and sipped a glass of orange juice while she waited for the bread to bake. She was getting eggs and butter from the refrigerator when she heard a series of crunching sounds outside. Someone was walking up to the cabin from the road. She deposited the eggs and butter on the cabinet and turned at the sound of footsteps on the porch. It would be Jake, coming to check on her. He'd probably come down from his cabin through the snow on his tractor. If she hadn't been so lost in thought, she would have heard the machine.

Thinking that he had arrived just in time to have a cup of coffee with her, she hurried to the door and swung it open, and the greeting she was about to utter died on her lips.

Thorne stood there. In the early morning light with the whiteness of the snow framing him, he looked dark and faintly menacing, although his expression was quite unreadable. He was wearing jeans and heavy boots with a sheepskin jacket and a gold muffler wound around his neck. His long legs were spread, his hands thrust deep into the side pockets of the jacket, the smooth blackness of his hair gleaming in the muted light.

Briefly panic gripped her. What was he doing here? How had he discovered where she was? Why couldn't he have let her alone for these few days?

She stood there, struggling to contain her panic, her breath coming shallow and quick. She felt an almost irresistible urge to run—as she had fled the New York apartment four years ago in the middle of the night, as she had run away from Oklahoma City the day before yesterday upon catching sight of Thorne. Surely there must be someplace where she could hide that he could not find her. She wasn't ready to face him yet.

But even as these thoughts raced through her mind, she knew that she could not evade him any longer. There was no place left to run to. Besides, he mustn't suspect that she was afraid to face him, for it might appear to him that such a fear was born of some deeper emotional reaction that he could still evoke in her.

"Rhea," he murmured quietly as she continued to stare at him. "May I come in? I'm freezing."

Dry-mouthed, she turned aside and walked back into the kitchen. She heard him stomping the snow from his boots at the door, and then the door closed. Her back to him, she gripped the back of one of the kitchen chairs, but after a moment she forced herself to turn toward him. He had moved to the hearth and stood, hands extended, warming himself at the fire. Then he unwound the muffler and removed his jacket, tossing them over one of the armchairs. He wore a heavy gray sweater over a navy shirt.

As she stood watching him, a log burned in two and fell crackling into the flames. It was the only sound in the cabin, and while at another time it would have reminded her that she was snug and warm and safe in her snowbound retreat, now it only lent a touch of unreality to the scene.

She watched Thorne's broad back and waited for him to say something. When it began to appear that he had no intention of doing so, she spoke raspingly into the ominous silence.

"How did you find me?"

He turned then, standing with his back to the fire, his hands clasped behind him. "After coming all the way from

New York, did you really think I'd let the matter of a few hundred miles of snowy roads stand in my way? You saw me outside your apartment night before last, didn't you? I stood there until very late before I realized you weren't coming. That's when I began to suspect that you'd seen me."

"Yes, I saw you," she declared, permitting her glance to meet his hard, penetrating look briefly. It was easy enough to tell herself that she would not let him see the misgiving and wariness she was feeling, but beneath Thorne's lancing regard she felt apprehension prickle along her veins. "Since you figured that out, I should think it would have been equally obvious that I didn't want to talk to you!"

He merely looked at her in silence for a few moments, and she was made aware once more of the changes she had seen in him two days earlier—scattered streaks of gray at the black temples, the gauntness in his rugged face, the disquieting, almost tormented look behind his implacable gaze. Was it possible that he had suffered, too? Tenderness stirred in her, but she clamped it down instantly. She knew too well Thorne's talent for taking advantage of small weaknesses. The only way to deal with him was with uncompromising bluntness. Nevertheless, her nerves shrieked for relief from the control she was exerting by the time he decided to answer her.

"What was obvious," said Thorne with relentless calm, "was that you had chosen, once again, to deal with an unpleasant situation by taking flight. This time I decided you wouldn't get away with it. Surely one meeting in four years is not too much to ask of my wife."

"I—I am not your wife," Rhea gasped indignantly. "Not in any way that counts."

"You are quite wrong. Legally you are still my wife, and

the law counts for a great deal in our society. Oh, I am aware that you are using your maiden name. At least, that's how I found you listed in the phone directory. But that doesn't change the fact that in actuality you are still Mrs. Thorne Folsom."

Rhea managed a sputter of contempt. "That doesn't give you the right to track me down like—"

"Very little tracking was required," he cut in curtly. "I went to the historical society. Your boyfriend Cragmont was less than helpful. He gave me a cock-and-bull story about your being out of town on a research project. It was obvious that he was lying. So I waited outside the building until quitting time and intercepted Clare Rutledge. Very accommodating woman, Clare. She was more than willing to have dinner with me."

Rhea could well believe it. Trusting Clare would have been flattered to be asked to dine with such a well-known author as Thorne Folsom. It wouldn't have entered her mind that he might have an ulterior motive in inviting her to dinner. "But—Clare didn't know where I'd gone."

"Oh, she told me that. She also said she wished she could help me, for she felt she owed me something in return for such a lovely dinner. Clare is a lonely woman. After a couple of drinks, she talked a blue streak. Of course, I had to sit through the story of her husband's last illness and death. But finally she confided that you weren't on assignment for the society at all but had asked for a few days' vacation. She thought that was odd because you hadn't said a word about wanting time off before you left and, besides, you always take your vacations during the summer months. She suspected you'd come to the cabin because, according to Clare, you spend all your vacations here." His glance left her face to wander about the room. "You've made it very attractive."

Rhea stilled an instinct to hug herself protectively. She should have known that Thorne would find her. When he wanted something badly enough, he got it. He could have found her at any time during the past four years, which only proved that he hadn't wanted to until now. He had probably found someone he wanted to marry and needed a quick divorce. Well, she would make it easy for him so that there would be no possible reason for him to stay long at the cabin.

As if to inspect the furnishings of the cabin more closely, he walked about the living area, touching a chair here, a maple commode there. Just when she thought she had a hold on her composure, he crossed the room and stopped mere inches from her.

"Well, Rhea," he murmured, raking a stray lock of dark hair from his eyes to look at her, "I've found you." His look sharpened as she gave in to the irresistible impulse to hug herself tightly, rubbing her hands along her sweatered arms. "Why are you afraid of me?"

"Afraid!" She made an indignant sound. "Don't be absurd! I don't imagine you are here to do me any physical harm."

His mouth twisted ironically. "Then why did you bolt when you saw me at your apartment?"

Rhea sighed. "I suppose it was the shock of seeing you again, and without any warning. I behaved irrationally. But you needn't have come to Oklahoma City at all, you know. A phone call would have served, preferably from your lawyer." She took a steadying breath and lifted her chin. "I've no intention of standing in the way of what you want, so—"

"Good!" His features hardened perceptibly as he cut her off in mid-spate. "Because what I want at the moment is food. I haven't eaten since before noon yesterday, and the smell coming from that oven is driving me crazy."

Rhea started and grabbed a pot holder from a drawer. "The biscuits!" She jerked open the oven door as a groan of exasperation escaped her. "Well, they're awfully brown, but still edible."

Thorne sat down at the small kitchen table, eyeing the egg carton on the cabinet. "Were you going to have eggs, too?"

She turned to transfer the biscuits to a napkin-lined straw basket. "Yes," she replied somewhat grudgingly, "and sausage links. Shall I scramble an egg for you?" He had always preferred his eggs scrambled, and a sideways glance at his expression told her he was getting some sort of sadistic satisfaction out of the fact that she had remembered.

"Please," he replied, "but make it three eggs, will you?" There was something unsettling in the way he was watching her every move. "All we need to make this breakfast perfect is strawberry jam. But since you had no idea I was coming, I'm probably out of luck there."

"It's in the refrigerator," she responded shortly as she broke eggs into a bowl.

"You've come to like it, too?" he queried. "I'm surprised. You used to swear by grape marmalade."

His long arm reached the jam without his moving from his chair. He continued to watch her silently while she prepared the sausage and eggs. The everyday activity became a monumental effort to appear calm, to move naturally. She was far too aware of the intense way he regarded her, and her nerves jangled with that awareness.

When she could prolong the preparations no longer, she had to sit facing him across the table and try to eat food that tasted like paper in her mouth and was almost as hard to swallow.

Thorne on the other hand ate with undisguised relish. Once she thought she noticed a slight tremor in his hand, but she put it down to hunger and admitted that he had been telling the truth when he said he hadn't eaten in almost twenty-four hours. That puzzled her, for she had never known Thorne to miss a meal before. He was a man of lusty appetites.

Forcing her mind away from that thought, she decided anything was better than the hovering silence at the table. If she were to reach an agreement with Thorne and be left alone again, the reason for this meeting must first be brought into the open.

She pushed her plate away and blurted, "I think we should talk about the divorce now."

From the corner of her eye she thought she saw his hand grip the knife beside his plate in a convulsive movement, but she might have imagined it. Certainly, when he spoke he did not sound disturbed, but merely weary. "I'm sorry, Rhea, but I'm too exhausted to talk about anything so serious now. I drove all night."

She was tempted to argue, but there was a certain stubbornness in the line of his jaw that she recognized. "I—I'm surprised your car didn't go off the road," she ventured.

He shrugged. "It did—between here and the spot where another vehicle—a small black foreign job—had gone into the ditch. Yours, I presume? I was lucky enough to find a four-wheel drive truck to rent in the city, which is why I got as far as I did."

Her hands gripped the sides of her chair seat and for a second her thoughts tumbled with renewed panic. He was stranded here, just as she was! He was looking at her, his body tensely waiting, as if he were preparing for her to become aware of their situation and protest. It was a frightening moment, a moment when his narrowed, black-lashed eyes gazed with blatant challenge into hers and, she was sure, saw the tremulous quality of her alarm. But she knew better than to voice her objections, for his leaving at the moment seemed to be utterly out of the question and he would like nothing better than to point that out to her. She forced her hands to relax and folded them in her lap, arranging her face in what she hoped was a composed expression, even though she was quaking inside.

"I see," she commented carefully.

"I would like to shower and have a nap, if you don't mind," he continued, still contemplating her.

With a small shrug of defeat, she began to clear the table. "I can hardly say no."

"I don't suppose you can. I'm rather stuck here at the moment. Even if I had the use of a vehicle, I'm too tired to drive anymore until I've rested."

Rhea licked her dry lips and carried their plates to the sink. "You know where the bathroom is," she said, her back to him.

His chair scraped against the tile as he got to his feet. "I'll just go back to the truck for my suitcase. I thought I'd better leave it until I saw whether you would let me through the door." He hesitated as if waiting for her to respond, which she refused to do. His seeming concern as to her reaction was nothing but a pose, and she knew it. After coming so far Thorne would have shoved his way in if she had tried to deny him entrance. He cleared his throat. "I intended to go on to my sister's later, but that's not possible now." He paused. "Thanks for the breakfast."

She ran hot water into the sink and added detergent. He put on his coat and muffler and left the cabin, and she finished clearing the table. She was rinsing the dishes and stacking them in a draining rack when he returned, and she did not even turn around until he had gone into the bedroom and shut the door behind him.

She finished in the kitchen and moved to the fireplace, where she sank into one of the armchairs and buried her face in her hands as she tried to force some semblance of form to thoughts and emotions that jumbled in a crazy quilt of disorder.

Thorne was still sleeping when Jake Sinclair arrived at eleven. Rhea heard his tractor some minutes before he was stomping the snow off his boots on the porch, and she put on another pot of coffee. She opened the door and greeted him warmly. With Thorne in the next room, the presence of the sturdy, white-haired man was even more comforting than it otherwise would have been.

"I've made us some coffee," she told him. "Take off your coat and sit down." She filled two large mugs and set them on the kitchen table.

Jake removed his snow-damp lumberjack's coat, spread it on the rug near the fire, and stradled the chair that Thorne had used earlier. "I see you're making out all right," he remarked as he pulled off his stocking cap and rubbed his leathery palms together. As she sat down across from him, the expression in his gray eyes was warm over the rim of the mug. "Where's your car?"

"In a ditch down the road about a half mile. I—I don't suppose you could pull it out with your tractor?" If he said yes, she would ask him to have a go at Thorne's truck, too.

He shook his head regretfully. "That's just a little garden tractor. Not enough power there to move a car—even a small one like yours."

She made a face. "I rather thought not. Well, I'd appreciate it if you would call for a wrecker when you get back to your cabin."

"I'll call," he told her, "but there's not much telling when they'll get around to you. From what I heard on the radio this morning, there are cars in ditches from here to McAlester. Looks like you're stranded for a few days." His scrutiny was thoughtful as she sighed, then lifted her mug to sip disconsolately. "Maggie sorta got the feeling you wanted to be alone for a spell, but if you get too lonely down here, you can always hike up to our place. We have that extra bedroom."

"Thanks, Jake, but I'll be fine." She smiled at him.

He nodded and took another swallow of coffee. Then he turned to glance over his shoulder toward the fireplace. Satisfied that his coat wasn't too close to the fire, he was bringing his gaze around to Rhea again when his head jerked back abruptly as he stared toward the couch. Following his gaze, Rhea saw Thorne's sheepskin jacket and the wool muffler folded over the back of the couch. The jacket could hardly be mistaken for a woman's, and evidently Jake didn't entertain that possibility, for a flush had crept into his face. He sipped at his coffee with studied nonchalance and avoided Rhea's gaze.

"Jake," she said uncomfortably, "I think there's something I should tell you."

"You don't have to tell me anything," he protested, clearly embarrassed. "I had no business opening my big yap about you being all alone down here, anyway. I didn't mean anything by it. I hope you know that, Rhea."

"Oh, I know you didn't," she assured him.

He grinned sheepishly and got to his feet, still without meeting her eyes. "I'll be getting along. Thanks for the coffee."

"My husband's here with me, Jake. He arrived this morning. He's in the next room sleeping."

105

Jake halted in his progress toward the fireplace to stare at her. "Thorne's *here*?"

She nodded a confirmation.

"Wait'll I tell Maggie!" He cocked his white head to one side and regarded her with a slightly reproving look. "And ain't you the sly one, though? Not a word when you called earlier." Jake and Maggie had met Thorne when he bought the cabin for Rhea. They had liked him immediately and the separation had not noticeably weakened their regard for him. Rhea would have had to be blind not to see the hopeful light that had come into Jake's gray eyes.

"Don't get the wrong idea," she said hastily. "I didn't expect him to come here. We haven't even had an opportunity to talk yet. But there's no chance of a reconciliation, Jake."

His shoulders slumped. "Are you sure, honey?"

"Yes," she told him.

"Well, tell him hello for me." He picked up his coat and put it on. At the door he added, "We'd like to see him if he'd care to come by before he leaves."

"I'll tell him, Jake."

When he was gone, Rhea had another cup of coffee and looked through the food supply to decide what to fix for lunch. There was a package of frozen noodles and some cans of chicken. Using a little imagination she combined these two ingredients in a casserole with peas, onion flakes, and a can of chicken soup, topping it off with buttered bread crumbs. She put it in the oven with corn muffins made from a mix. Then she made egg custard for dessert.

As long as she could keep herself occupied in the kitchen, there was less opportunity to think of Thorne and the coming "talk," which, no matter how long she had to get used to the idea, she could not contemplate without some trepidation. But surely, she told herself, it would be brief, for she would agree to whatever terms he named. Actually, she didn't want a financial settlement. Her salary was enough for her to live on, and she didn't feel that her three months with Thorne entitled her to any of his money. Oh, yes, she meant to make it very easy for him to be free of her.

When the casserole and bread were done, she placed them on a warming board and covered them with a tea towel. At one there still had been no sound from the bedroom. By that time she had been keeping the food warm for an hour, and she didn't know how much longer lunch could be postponed. Soon the food would be dried out and tasteless.

After long moments of indecision, she went to the bedroom door and tapped lightly. There was no reply, and so she turned the knob and looked into the room. Thorne was sprawled diagonally across the bed on his back. He had not changed his sleeping habits, she thought with a queer stab of regret. They had had a king-sized bed in New York, but still she had had to curl her body into the small spaces Thorne's sprawling form had left unoccupied. She had not minded in the least, for she would have slept with her body entwined with Thorne's, no matter how much room they had. She had loved waking up to the sensuous comfort of his warm skin touching hers.

As she watched, his head moved and his arm thrashed out, flinging back the covers, exposing his bare, muscled chest and the white waistband of his undershorts. The movement stilled one of her misgivings, anyway, for Thorne usually slept in the raw. He turned onto his side, his face pressing into the pillow, and mumbled incoherently.

Something was wrong, she realized. She went to the bedside and spoke his name, but he did not respond. In the light from the window, she saw that there was an unhealthy gray pallor beneath the deep tan of his skin and beads of perspiration stood on his forehead. She stood there, feeling helpless for a moment, and then tentatively touched her fingers to his cheek. His skin felt cold and clammy.

She began trying to disentangle the bedclothes and cover him.

"What—?" His voice startled her. She straightened and looked into his face. He was trying to sit up, watching her with an uncomprehending expression, his dark eyes glazed. She pulled the bedclothes up to his shoulders.

"You've thrown the covers off, Thorne. Lie still."

He closed his eyes and slumped back against the pillows. He looked so fatigued, as if his thrashing about had exhausted him. It was difficult to believe that such an evidently serious illness had come on so suddenly.

"Thorne? Were you feeling ill before you arrived here?"

He shook his head slowly without opening his eyes. "I'm all right," he uttered thickly. "Just a little achy. Sorry . . . to cause . . . trouble."

He turned his face aside, his breath escaping in a soft, rasping sound. From that angle the unhealthy sheen of the skin of his face and neck was more noticeable. Rhea guessed that he must not have felt entirely well before leaving Oklahoma City, and the strain of the long drive had drained his strength. No doubt the loss of sleep and exposure to the cold had worsened his condition. Thorne's stubbornness would kill him one day, she thought desperately, for she was certain he would have come after her had he been shaking with fever—as perhaps he had been. Common sense argued that he had brought this upon himself, but nevertheless compassion urged her to comfort him.

"You're not causing trouble," she said, sensing that she ought to at least ease his mind about that. "Is there anything I can do for you?" She tucked the bedclothes more tightly about his shoulders and realized for the first time that he was shaking.

"I'm—cold," he muttered, his jaw clamped to stop his teeth from chattering.

Although the room temperature felt comfortable to her, she turned up the heater and got the two extra blankets from the closet and spread them over him.

Turning his head he looked at her with heavy eyes that held the glitter of illness and something more, a sort of pleading. She could not resist the urge to tuck the bedclothes even more closely around him, smoothing them out as she did so. He closed his eyes again, expelling a deep sigh. She looked for a long moment into his face—at the faint dark stubble on his chin, the sunken hollows beneath the high cheekbones where the thick black lashes rested, at the strong, masculine nose, and she was assailed by a near-overpowering need to smooth the dark tangle of hair back from his forehead.

She left the room quickly, leaving the door ajar so that she could hear if he called her. She had lunch and rummaged through the food supply until she found a container of bouillon packets. She laid one of the packets on the table for preparation when Thorne awoke. He probably would not feel like eating, but he must have liquids to prevent dehydration. Then she tried, without much success, to read a magazine she had brought with her.

In midafternoon she heard Thorne thrashing about again and found him burning with fever. She brought him aspirin and helped him into a half-sitting position so that he could swallow them with a full glass of water. She turned the heater down again and folded back the two blankets she had added when he was chilling.

When she straightened, she realized that he was watching her intently. "Thorne?" she murmured, coming around to the head of the bed. "Are you feeling any better?"

"This room feels like an oven." He moved to thrust back more of the bedclothes. "Can't you open a window?"

"No, it's freezing out," she told him gently. "But I've turned down the heater and taken away some of the blankets. It's the fever that's making you feel so warm."

"Oh." His dark brows drew together, and he reached out to grasp her hand. His fingers felt scaldingly hot, and when she tried to extricate herself, he only gripped tighter. Her instinctive withdrawal caused a spasm of something —anger or bewilderment—to cross his face.

"Rhea . . ." The sheen of his dark eyes was far too bright to be normal. "Don't leave me here alone. Sit beside me, please."

"Thorne—"

Rhea was feeling the fluttering of panic closing in on her. His weakened state was causing her to feel too much tenderness and compassion, and yet she couldn't be hard enough to leave him when he pleaded so pathetically.

Still, she tried. "Thorne, I'll be right in the next room."

His fingers gripped hers painfully. "No! I want you here."

He was becoming agitated, and she didn't know what he might do if she refused him. With a feeling of helplessness she lowered herself slowly to sit on the bed.

"Thank you . . ." He sank back against the pillows and his fingers relaxed, although they remained curled around her own. Within moments he was asleep, and she removed

110

his fingers gently and pulled the sheet and one blanket over his chest before she tiptoed across the room.

As she reached the door, he cried out raspingly, "Rhea!" She turned around, thinking that he had awakened and found her gone. But he was not awake. He was turning on the pillow, muttering to himself, and then he called her name a second time. Somehow his calling for her in delirium—the seeming vulnerability of it—touched her deeply.

She hesitated on the threshold for several moments, trying to decide if she should leave him to hike to the Sinclairs' cabin, where she could phone for a doctor. Walking for a mile uphill through deep snow would take a half hour, at least. And even if she found a doctor who would be willing to make a house call, there would be slight chance of his reaching them.

From Thorne's symptoms and what he had said about feeling achy, she thought he had the flu, for which a doctor would tell her to give him aspirin and fluids and keep him in bed. This she was doing already. She decided to wait until later and go to the Sinclairs only if he seemed worse.

Chapter 6

When he awoke at six, she felt reassured that she had made the right decision in not going for help. His fever was down and he seemed better.

"I'll bring you more aspirin," she told him. "It should keep your temperature from rising again."

"I can wait on myself," he muttered, sitting up. "If you will hand me my robe from the suitcase . . ."

She hesitated. "Don't you think you should stay in bed?"

"No," he stated flatly. "My robe, please."

Sighing, she located the heavy tan robe and a pair of leather house slippers. She watched him climb unsteadily from the bed, and then as he hesitated seemingly overcome by light-headedness, she helped him into the robe and tied the belt about his waist. He watched her with heavy-lidded eyes, and looking away, she took the slippers and, with some reservation, put an arm around his waist to help him into the other room.

He sat on the couch and put on the slippers while she

regarded him worriedly. Then he laid his head against the back of the couch and looked up at her.

"Do you feel as if you could eat something? Some bouillon or soup?" she asked, thinking that he appeared to have lost another five pounds since his arrival.

His gaze was clearer now. "I don't want to put you to any more trouble."

She knew that ordinarily he disliked being dependent on anyone, but there was no way of knowing whether he truly regretted the inconvenience his illness might be causing or if he was secretly enjoying her having to wait on him. His hand came up slowly to run across his face, as if he were clearing away clinging cobwebs. Seeing the slight tremor in the hand caused by the weakness that follows fever, she regretted her uncharitable thoughts.

"You must have some nourishment to get well."

"And out of your hair?" he inquired.

Whatever answer she made to that would lead to pitfalls that were better avoided, and so she made none. She brought him aspirin and a glass of water, then decided he seemed well enough to eat something a little more substantial than bouillon. She heated vegetable soup and set it with crackers and hot tea on a tray, which she carried to him. While he ate, she changed the sheets on his bed.

When she had finished in the bedroom, he had eaten everything on the tray. "Your appetite's returning. That's a good sign." She stood in front of the fireplace, facing him. "You shouldn't have made that drive when you were ill."

"I didn't feel ill when I left," he grumbled. "I guess I've let myself get run-down."

Rhea's lips pressed together to hold back a caustic agreement. She knew that he was "run-down" because of the unwise manner in which he had lived since their separation. The scandal sheets made it sound as if his life had been one long round of parties and women. She knew such stories were exaggerated, but there must be some truth in what she had read. Where there was smoke, there was fire, and the poorer quality of his work the last few years seemed to confirm that.

His expression was ironic, as if he could read her thoughts. She decided it was not a good time to bring up the divorce again. "Do you want to go back to bed?"

He leaned forward and stretched out a hand to touch her arm. She flinched away from him, but his fingers curved around her wrist, imprisoning it.

"Won't you sit down and talk to me?" he asked, tightening his hold as she tried to free herself. Her heartbeat quickened at the satyric way he was regarding her.

"Thorne, I have to do the dishes . . ." she breathed shakily, as an electric attraction assailed her senses. Sitting there with his robe covering too little of his bare chest and muscled legs, he exerted a sexuality that almost took her breath away. She had forgotten how strong a pull his look and touch could have on her senses. But it had always been that way with her and Thorne, and she supposed she shouldn't be surprised that the attraction could still be there, even after love had gone. She was a normal woman and one who had held herself aloof from men for four years.

"Thorne, please let go of me."

He continued to look into her eyes for a long moment, and then his hand dropped away. "Very well. I guess you still find it distasteful to be near me. I only thought there might be a few good memories, enough to allow you to talk to me with some civility. Well, go on about your business. I'll try to stay out of your way."

"Oh, Thorne . . ." Rhea sighed hopelessly.

114

He sounded so dejected, looked so weak. She managed to stifle the thought that he was still a master at manipulating her. With considerable qualms she lowered herself to the couch. "I don't mean to be insensitive. You're right. We have to be able to talk to each other or the next few days will be intolerable."

"As soon as I feel stronger," he said, staring into the fire, "I'll go up to the Sinclairs and call Gracie. Maybe she can come for me."

Now Rhea was certain that he was appealing to her sympathy. "You can't do that. It's much too dangerous to ask your sister to drive out here—at least, not until the roads improve."

He moved restlessly. After a moment he said, "It's very comforting here. I'd forgotten. And you've done wonders with the place."

"I enjoyed doing it," she told him, relieved to have the conversation take a less personal direction. "This is my real home, even though I spend much less time here than in the apartment. If I could find a job nearby, I think I'd come here to live."

He looked at her in an odd way. "Would you? You wouldn't miss the city and your friends there?"

"I might," she confessed. "But some of my high-school classmates still live in Idabel. I could renew old acquaintances."

His brows drew together. "Have you ever brought anyone to the cabin?"

"A few times I've invited friends for the weekend. Mostly, I prefer being alone here. I almost think I could be content with a reclusive life. Perhaps there is more of my grandfather in me than I ever imagined."

He hunched his shoulders. "Is Don Cragmont one of the 'friends' who's been here with you?"

Rhea had started to relax, thinking that maybe the few days they would have to spend together might be bearable, after all. But at the abrupt question all her defenses came up again. "I don't like being interrogated, Thorne, any more than you would like it if I started questioning you about your life and your—women."

He sat very still for a moment and then he pulled his robe together over his chest. "It seems colder."

She got up and lifted logs from the hearth basket to build up the fire again. Noticing a slight tremor pass through him, she bent to touch his forehead. He felt overly warm, but it was too soon for more aspirin. "I'll bring you a blanket."

He captured her hand. "No." Feeling trapped and helpless, she allowed him to pull her down on the couch again. Sighing, he relaxed against the padded arm of the couch and brought her palm to his warm lips. His mouth pressed gently against her sensitive skin and the imprint seemed to sear the flesh.

His arms encircled her, pressing her close to him. "You can keep me much warmer than a blanket," he muttered, his breath hot against her cheek. He was trembling and she wondered wildly if it was caused by his illness or overheated emotions.

She allowed herself to relax against him, strangely reluctant to move away. If she resisted, he might become agitated and that would not be good for him, she reasoned. Yet she also realized that a part of her welcomed the warmth of his embrace. It had been so long since she had felt his arms around her, so very long . . .

"That's better," he murmured softly. His trembling had subsided, and she knew she ought to pull away now but she didn't. She lay very still, her head resting on his shoulder, and breathed in the earthy, masculine smell of his skin. The feverish warmth of his body was penetrating hers, infusing her with a drowsy limpness that seemed to spread throughout her body. If only time could stop at that moment . .

Good Lord, what was she thinking? Was she insane? Squirming, she tried to rise from the couch. His arms tightened around her.

"Rhea, Rhea . . ." His lips moved against the smooth skin of her forehead with excruciating intimacy. "Stay with me for a little while—until I feel warmer."

Cursing herself for a weak coward, she gave in. Sensing her capitulation, Thorne sighed contentedly, his warm breath ruffling her hair, and his hand moved over her back in an intimate caress.

She closed her eyes and allowed herself to enjoy the gentling pleasure of his fingers tracing the contours of her back through the sweater she wore. What did it matter if she permitted him to hold her one last time? Why shouldn't she draw what comfort she could from his need for her—even if it was a need born of illness?

From comfort it was but a short step to desire. Thorne's hands continued to stroke her body, his arms pressing her so tightly against him that she could hear the deep throbbing of his heart. And slowly her starving senses, so long smothered and denied, began to come quiveringly to life. Her fingers gently traced the hard line of his collarbone, and a profound longing burst the tight bounds that she had managed to impose upon her emotions for years and to spread throughout cell and sinew until her blood pulsed with awareness and yearning. Dear God, how could she still want him, after all that he had done?

His hands became quiet, his arms relaxing the grip that had held her. Her face flushed, she lifted her head to look into his face. His eyes were closed and, from the deep even rhythm of his breathing, she knew that he had fallen asleep.

Carefully, she moved out of his embrace. He settled into a more comfortable position, mumbling quietly in his sleep.

Rhea got to her feet, still profoundly shaken, and stood looking down at him. She felt hot as the passion that had been crying out for assuagement gradually quieted, leaving her feeling weak and foolish. For a moment she had been willing to forget everything for the satisfaction of the needs that Thorne's touch had awakened in her. If he had not fallen asleep . . .

Her hands came up to cover her face, and she turned away from the sight of him as the beginning of self-knowledge flooded through her. It had been more than physical desire that she had felt, something deeper, more meaningful. In spite of everything could she still love him? Was that the explanation for the abject fear that had struck her at the mere sight of him two days ago and again that morning when she opened the door to him? Did she fear him because subconsciously she had known how feeble, in the face of love, were the defenses built by wounded pride and humiliation?

It was true, all of it. The knowledge was like a steel hand clamping down on her chest. May heaven help her, for if heaven did not she didn't know how she would survive the next few days.

Later, rather than disturb Thorne's sleep, Rhea covered him with blankets and left him on the couch for the night. It was quite late before she could relax enough to sleep in the bed that Thorne had so recently vacated.

Once she drifted off, though, she slept soundly and without any dreams disturbing enough to linger in memory upon awaking. When she awoke, pale winter sunlight fell through the window to warm her face. She shifted her position so that the sunlight no longer touched her and snuggled more deeply into the bed, wanting to reenter the lovely imperturbability of sleep.

Then she heard pans rattling in the kitchen. She sat up reluctantly as she smelled brewing coffee. Knowing she would not sleep again, she went into the bathroom to freshen up before dressing hurriedly in khaki jeans and a yellow oxford-cloth shirt. Entering the kitchen moments later, she found Thorne, still in robe and slippers, buttering freshly made toast. He smiled at her, and although he evidently felt a great deal better, he still looked too weak and haggard to be fixing breakfast.

"I was going to serve your breakfast in bed, but since you're up, sit down. I'll have it ready in a minute."

After a brief hesitation, she obeyed. "You shouldn't overexert yourself."

"Let me be the judge of what is too much exertion, okay?"

He spooned steaming oatmeal into bowls and set them on the table with the platter of toast. Then he poured the coffee and joined her.

She busied herself adding butter and honey to the hot cereal. A tentative taste confirmed that it was cooked to perfection, creamy and smooth in her mouth.

"You've learned to cook," she observed.

He reached for a piece of toast. "I've learned a lot of things during the past four years." There was a guarded look in the eyes that met hers.

Thinking she understood the reason for his grim tone, she said, "I—I'm sorry for the trouble you've had with the critics. I don't think they've been entirely fair."

His look sharpened on her face. "Have you read my last two books?"

"Yes," she admitted.

"And?"

"Well, I'm sure I'm not the best judge, but I—I liked the earlier novels better." He seemed to be waiting for her to elaborate. "Maybe it's because you've dealt with non-Indian themes more recently and I found it harder to identify with the characters. The writing seemed to lack . . . conviction." She halted, fearing she had said too much. "As I say, I'm certainly not qualified to judge."

"On the contrary," he responded, "you've gone right to the heart of the matter—or perhaps I should say to the heart of the author. As much as I dislike admitting it, the critics have made some valid points, even though I think they've gone a bit overboard by dragging in my personal life—or what they imagine is my personal life."

"It's been painful for you, hasn't it?" she ventured, moved by his honesty.

"Very," he replied shortly. "But, at last, I've come to realize what I have to do. I'm not going back to New York to live—ever. I began to lose contact with myself in that environment, and the two years in California hastened the process. I thought, when I left the West Coast, if I went back to New York . . ." His voice trailed off.

"Where do you plan to live?"

"Here—in Oklahoma," he told her. "I should never have left. I've found it difficult to concentrate on my work during the past year, but once I made the decision to come home, something loosened inside me. The flow I used to have in the early books is back. Sometimes I write for twelve and fifteen hours at a stretch because the story seems to be pushing to come out. Maybe that's because

I've gone back to my roots. I'm writing that Choctaw generational saga I once told you about."

How vivid that evening was in her memory! She had made dinner for them after his autograph party at the historical society, and he had told her of his desire to combine some of the tragedy, courage, and joy of their people into a book—a novel that would crown his career with the finest writing of which he was capable and perhaps live on long after him. There had been the same ring of conviction in his voice that she heard there now. Regardless of what had happened between them, she wanted him to write that book, knowing that it was essential to his sense of having discharged a duty laid on him by his conscience and his talent.

"Oh, Thorne—I'm glad. You told me you would know when the time was right to begin that book, and it's wonderful that it's come just now when—"

His mouth twisted in an expression of cynicism. "In time to save my career? No, don't apologize. It's true. It's quite likely that it has also saved my sanity."

She searched for evidence of mockery in his face and found none. "I know the book's important, but as for your sanity—I doubt I've ever met anyone as emotionally strong as you."

His eyes deepened to a lackluster black, as if his thoughts were painful. "You don't know what the last four years have been like for me."

Without thinking she responded gravely, "They haven't been a bed of roses for me, either."

"Haven't they?" he inquired quietly. "I would have thought you were giddy with relief at being rid of me."

"Hardly giddy." She began to clear the table, carrying dishes to the sink in order to avoid meeting his look. With her back to him she added, "I couldn't take the failure of my marriage so lightly, even though there was no other alternative." She turned to face him and said briskly, "But that's all water under the bridge now, isn't it?"

His reply was noncommittal. "It would seem so." His black eyes seemed to bore into hers. "Although I've never understood how I could have misread you so completely. I thought you were relatively content and then—" He halted, seeing the withdrawal in her face. "Apparently," he continued on a less intense note, "the only thing I did right was to give you this cabin. Now I find I envy you your retreat. It would be the perfect place to finish my book. I don't suppose you would allow me the use of it for the remainder of the winter." Seeing her alarm, he uttered a short, humorless laugh. "No, I thought not."

"I—I'm sure there are other cabins in the area that you could rent," she faltered. She turned her attention to the task of cleaning up the kitchen, going to the table again to remove his empty cup. Then, hesitatingly and without quite meeting his gaze, she asked, "Would you care for more coffee?"

"No, thank you." Just as her fingers began to curl around the cup handle, he grasped her arm and with one swift tug unbalanced her so that she was pulled onto his lap. His other hand slid around her waist, exerting enough strength to keep her from rising. "It's not coffee that I want."

Beneath his hands, she began to struggle. "Let me go," she protested breathlessly. He gripped her chin with one hand and forced her face around to meet his. His kiss was hard, the force of it bending her backward against his arm. There was no gentleness in him, only hunger. It was a demanding, invading kiss that crushed her lips apart and penetrated the warmth of her mouth with a ruthless determination that left her faint and unreasoning. Her arms gripped his shoulders and clung as if to draw strength from the only solid thing in the world. His hands slid down her back and brought her against his hard body. Through her clothing his masculine contours burned her flesh with searing awareness.

For a moment she forgot that this could not happen. Her conscious mind knew only the bruising hunger of his kiss and his body, and the bittersweet longing stirring in her—but only for a moment. Then she was joltingly aware of where this was leading and tore her lips from his. His eyes opened slowly, night-dark, unsmiling, heavy with unsated passion.

Breathing raggedly she stared at him for a long moment. Distrust invaded the burning depths of his eyes and his mouth thinned. When he spoke, his words were unexpected and cold. "Why don't you want to let me use the cabin? Is it because you want to keep bringing Cragmont here?"

Feeling his grip relaxing, she jerked away, freeing her pinioned body and coming to her feet. She caught her lip between her teeth, then said tremblingly, "That is none of your business."

She turned away from him and took the few steps required to bring her next to the cabinet, where she gripped the edge and stared down at the marbleized Formica covering. The silence was pregnant with unuttered resentment and old pain. The graceful swirls in the Formica seemed to swim before Rhea's eyes and bitter rancor loosened her tongue. "What does Diane Lowery think of your decision to leave New York?"

After a long pause he replied tersely, "I haven't the least idea. I've had another agent for almost two years. I haven't even seen Diane in more than a year."

So, thought Rhea, *he finally broke whatever hold Diane*

had on him. In a former time, the knowledge would have brought satisfaction. Now that it was much too late it seemed of little significance.

"Rhea—"

The anger in his voice had given way to a subdued note. She reined her emotions enough to face him. Turning around, she leaned back against the cabinet and waited, her face set and still.

"Why did you leave me without a word of explanation? Didn't you owe me that much?"

"*Owe you?* I can't believe you said that!"

"You didn't even have the decency to face me with whatever was bothering you."

"*Decency!*" Her teeth grated, her voice thick with the lancing pain of that night four years earlier and Thorne's cruel betrayal. "You have the gall to speak to me of decency!"

He did not move, but his chilling regard held her immobile, as surely as if he had pinned her with his hands. "You will explain what you mean by that—please." The last word was not touched by any hint of request; rather it was a command.

A short, near-hysterical laugh escaped her. "Can you really imagine that I was in any state to *talk* after finding you in bed with Diane?" Her voice rasped in the tense silence of the cabin. "My God, I couldn't even bear to look at you!"

He had come slowly to his feet, the table a barrier between them. He stared at her, a look of mingled shock and bewilderment on his face. "You found me in bed with Diane?" He said the words slowly as if they were foreign sounds with no meaning for him.

She shook her head as if to clear her thoughts. "You don't even remember, do you? You were too drunk."

He took a step toward her but stopped as she stiffened against the cabinet. She saw a pulse beating at the base of his throat, and his hands clenched and unclenched at his sides. "I don't know what you're talking about."

She shrugged, but she could not dispel the weight of hopelessness. "Does it matter now?"

"It matters to me," he snapped. "Tell me what you think happened that night—all of it."

She shook her head again. "Let it alone, Thorne."

"Tell me!" He was blocking her way, his stance and his tone implacable and unyielding.

He *didn't* remember and to Rhea's inflamed emotions that seemed to make his casting aside of his marriage vows even worse. He couldn't even recall what had been the most painful experience of her life!

"I know you were angry with me when I left to meet Diane that night," he said after a moment. "I had no idea how angry until later."

"Yes, I was angry," she said, the words hard-edged with defiance. "I went to an all-night movie house. After a while I started to think I'd been unfair, so I went back to the apartment." She met his look, her eyes clouding with remembered agony. "Diane was just leaving the bedroom. She was still trying to get back into her clothes."

He ran shaking fingers through his hair. "Let me see if I understand this. You *saw* Diane leaving my bedroom half dressed?"

"Yes," she said, hardly above a whisper.

"What did she say to you?"

Rhea closed her eyes briefly, then stared through the kitchen window at the virgin bleakness of the snow that blanketed and smoothed the outlines of everything in sight. "She said that I was bound to find out sooner or later. She said you told her I was away on a holiday or she would have taken you somewhere besides my bed." She glanced back at him, her face set rigidly. "Frankly, I think that was a lie. She was glad I walked in when I did. She probably knew I was too besotted to believe you capable of such deliberate cruelty if I hadn't seen it with my own eyes."

His jaw hardened dangerously. The sound he made was harsh with outrage. "But you didn't see anything, you little fool! How could you have let Diane dupe you so easily? You wouldn't have if you had trusted me. I told you before we were married that Diane was nothing to me."

"She said that you were lovers, that you always came back to her," Rhea retorted, enraged by his accusatory tone. "I refused to believe her until I had no other choice."

"You read the worst into what you saw because at the gut level you always doubted me! Diane must have sensed that, and she used it. She manipulated both of us."

"You're not going to stand there and tell me she seduced you!" Rhea cried contemptuously.

"No, I'm telling you that nothing happened between Diane and me that night. Don't you understand yet?" His shoulders slumped and he lowered himself to the chair that he had left moments before. For a second he held his head in his hands, as if he were trying to gather his waning strength. Then he looked at her, his expression profoundly melancholy.

"Oh, I can't put all the blame on Diane. I'd had too much to drink. To be perfectly honest, I can recall only fragments of the events of that night. The meeting with the film company representatives went on for hours. I lost track of how many drinks I'd had. It wasn't until later that I realized Diane had deliberately prolonged the meeting by bringing up minor points for negotiation. To the best of my recollection, it was Diane, too, who kept ordering new rounds of drinks."

At the disbelieving look in Rhea's eyes his mouth twisted. "I know—I could have called a halt. But I didn't. I was worried about leaving you alone when you were obviously upset, and maybe I was trying to blot out the guilt feelings. By the time the meeting broke up, I was unsteady on my feet. Diane insisted on seeing me home. When we got to the apartment, you weren't about. I believe I assumed you were still angry with me and had gone to bed in the guest room."

"I remember that Diane found my fumbling efforts to take off my tie amusing. She steered me toward the bedroom and helped me out of my clothes. She assured me she would explain everything to you before she left. After that—my memory is a blank. I am very sure, however, that I did not make love to Diane. She must have waited until she heard you returning and then 'set the scene' for what followed. The next thing I remember, I woke up with a blinding headache. It was after noon. I got up and went in search of you. I found your note instead. It crossed my mind briefly that Diane might have said something to make you even angrier at me than you had been before. But when I questioned her, she said she hadn't even seen you the night before, that you weren't in the apartment when she left. I had no idea the lengths to which she would go—"

Rhea had listened to this recital with growing disbelief. Now she hugged herself in an effort to still the shaking that had invaded her body. "And you didn't even try to find me, to try to explain?"

He eyed her with a look of stubbornness about his mouth. "I was too angry at first, and hurt because you had so little interest in preserving our marriage that you wouldn't even come to me and discuss our problems. I thought you would come back once you'd had time to think things through. When I didn't hear from you, I finally telephoned. I was ready to apologize, to beg you to come back—but you were so cold and distant. You would hardly talk to me. It seemed obvious you wanted nothing more to do with me." His tone hardened. "I guess Cragmont had already moved into the breach. So I didn't say any of the things I had intended."

Rhea's thoughts were in total confusion. How could she believe him? If he couldn't remember that night, how could he be so sure he hadn't made love to Diane? And if he had really cared for her, would he have given up so easily? He had surely found quick consolation in other arms. It was this final thought that stiffened her resolve. "Even if what you say about Diane is true," she retorted, "you wasted no time in finding other women to take my place."

He was looking at her with disdain, all other emotion rigidly tamped down. "I don't mean to apologize for the way I lived my life after you left me. You've already had more than your pound of flesh from me, Rhea."

His accusation was like icy water thrown into her face. They regarded each other in wordless anger for several moments until Thorne got to his feet again. "I'm going to bed," he stated and started for the bedroom. Part way there, he turned back. On his face there was a proud, defiant expression. "If you'll be honest with yourself, you'll realize that Diane wasn't the real problem. Maybe you were right when you said our marriage was a mistake from the beginning."

The confrontation must have drained the remainder of Thorne's strength. He slept through the day—or at least rested quietly in bed—while Rhea tried to keep busy about the cabin. She carried in wood from the porch, stacking it in the hearth basket. She swept the kitchen and living room and dusted all the furniture. She made stew and cobbler from canned peaches. Nevertheless, she found herself with too much idle time on her hands, time in which she recalled everything Thorne had said earlier in the kitchen and felt trapped and hopelessly confused.

When dusk had fallen, she made her way quietly through the darkened bedroom where Thorne slept, bound for the bathroom and a hot shower. Minutes later she emerged from the shower stall and, after drying herself, wrapped her velour robe about her. Standing in front of the small steam-fogged mirror, she brushed her hair vigorously. Rather than disturb Thorne, she decided to sleep on the couch. She reentered the bedroom, intending to take her gown from the closet and go into the living room to put it on.

She found Thorne sitting on the side of the bed. In spite of a firm resolution her senses raced at the sight of his bare, lean body clad only in his undershorts. She looked quickly away from his brown skin, and determined to ignore the intimacies of their enforced confinement together, she said, "You've had a long rest. Are you feeling any better?"

"Not particularly," he muttered, his dark eyes lost in the shadowy dimness of the room.

"You'd better get back into bed then," she said, forcing a businesslike tone into her voice that she was far from feeling. "I'll bring your dinner on a tray." To emphasize her words, she went to the bed and pulled back the rumpled bedcovers to smooth them. "Get in and I'll cover you."

Thorne swung his legs back onto the bed, and she pulled the covers over him. But when she would have moved away, he caught her hand. "Hmmm, you've just come from the shower, haven't you? You smell lovely." She found herself staring into his eyes.

"Thorne, don't . . ."

She pulled on her hand, trying to avoid his searching look. He seemed to have regained his strength with amazing rapidity, for she found herself half lying across the bed, crushed against him. The contact, even with the bedclothes between them, made her aware of her own lack of defenses. Somehow she had to hide that from him, but held so close against him, her body clamoring for an even more intimate contact, she found it difficult to pretend indifference.

"Rhea," he whispered roughly against her hair, "don't keep pushing me away. You want me to hold you, don't you? I can feel your body trembling when I touch you."

"No, I—" But her denial was cut short by the pressure of his mouth, and her fragile resistance collapsed beneath his feverish strength. And when his kiss deepened and gentled with such seductive tenderness, she felt her body molding itself to the shape of his and tingling with excitement. His hands moved to the belt of her robe, loosening and releasing it, then pushed the garment off her shoulders. His mouth left hers to find the warm swollen mound of her breast, and instead of protesting, she found her arms cradling his head and pressing him even closer.

"You are still mine, Rhea—" he murmured thickly as he shifted the bedcovers to pull her naked body against his. She knew that she should deny his possession, but her overheated emotions had taken over and she could not.

As his body moved to cover hers, she lay unresisting as tears—of regret or happiness, she couldn't tell—slid silently down her cheeks. He kissed her wet lashes and cheeks with infinite tenderness and murmured the same endearments that had disturbed her dreams for years. Gradually his kisses became more demanding and, slowly, she responded with a hunger of her own. She had no thought of the consequences of what she was doing, nor did she care that he was proving the truth of his claim to ownership. Not then. She was too lost in the rampage of her own emotions and all that mattered was that this man—the only man who had ever touched her heart—should go on caressing her, loving her until the fire of her passion was dampened by the assuagement that only he could give.

Then she was caressing the masculine hardness of his body, so long lost to her, and moving against him with an abandon that would have shocked her had she been able to think coherently. She wanted only to experience the sweet joining of their bodies, to possess and be possessed in return, to feel after all the years that ultimate physical fulfillment and the easing of the demand of all her senses. . . .

Chapter 7

The cabin was enclosed in a cocoon of nighttime silence. Inside, lamplight dulled the earth tones of the Navaho rug and the red of the armchairs. Having left the bed and fumbled into her robe in an agony of self-recrimination for what she had allowed to happen, Rhea sat on the couch and tried to erase the image of herself in Thorne's arms. It was futile, of course.

"You wanted it as much as I did."

She looked over her shoulder to see Thorne in his tan robe, standing in the bedroom doorway. Since a denial of the statement was impossible, she stared at the hands lying in her lap and did not answer.

Thorne moved to the hearth and looked down at her bent head. "You've been crying."

Again, a reply seemed superfluous. In the silence a chunk of ice fell from the eave of the cabin and landed outside near the front porch, the sound muffled by the snow.

"Talk to me, Rhea!"

Black lashes, tangled and damp, lifted and she looked at him impassively. "What shall we talk about, Thorne? The weather? Or perhaps you would like to point out how I compare with your other lovers in bed."

His expression contorted in a dangerous scowl. "Damn it! Why can't you admit that we're as good together as we ever were?"

What he said was true. The chemistry was as strong as ever, stronger than she would have believed possible, but it was so much less than she wanted. There could be no man-woman relationship without chemistry, but if chemistry was all there was, it could be worse than nothing. It was possible, she supposed, to be sexually attracted to someone whom one despised. That was one of those human paradoxes that could not be understood—except perhaps by psychiatrists. But in the end such a relationship could only degrade.

"Physical compatibility is hardly a rare thing. You, of all men, should know that." Humiliation blunted the words and drove her to add, "So tell me, on a scale of one to ten, how do I rate with Diane and the others? Am I a five? A six?"

A muttered curse escaped him as he jerked her to her feet and shook her. "Stop it, Rhea! It's more than—"

Fiercely she wrenched from his grasp and turned her back on him. "You needn't waste your breath trying to be kind!" Her voice shook. "If you had ever really cared, you would have come after me four years ago. If I'd thought you had any real feelings for me, I'd have contacted you when I learned I was—" She halted abruptly, belatedly aware that shame had pushed her almost too far. She turned to face him, desperate to return to safe ground. "Nothing can be gained by rehashing it all again."

Her glance wavered under his keen regard. "What did you start to say?"

"I don't know what you mean."

He cut her off. "Yes, you do. You would have contacted me when you learned you were what?"

She looked away from him, seeking to escape those brightly penetrating eyes. "I'm tired, Thorne. We'll talk things out later, when you're completely well." A note of pleading had crept unwanted into her tone.

He grasped her arm roughly and whirled her about. "Tell me," he ground out.

He had never looked more arrogant, and she almost hated him for his unfeeling determination to have his own way. He meant to force an answer from her. Blood pounded in Rhea's head as his grip on her arm tightened threateningly. She saw the futility of further procrastination, and perhaps she wanted to hurt him, too, as he had hurt her.

She sucked in her breath. "When—when I learned I was pregnant," she exclaimed tremulously. "I discovered it a few days after I left you. The one time you telephoned me, I'd just left the hospital, and I was still rather unsteady emotionally."

He released his hold on her arm, as if he feared he might do her injury otherwise. "There was a miscarriage?" He spoke quietly, but there was a hint of menace, too.

Her eyes widened as a suspicion crept into her thoughts. "Of course there was a miscarriage! You can't think I'd have an abortion!"

His look was measuring, as if he was weighing the truth of her words. Finally he said, "You'd been gone more than a month when I phoned. That means you knew of the pregnancy some weeks before the miscarriage. Why

134

wasn't I told? Am I to assume that you thought the news would be of no interest to me?"

"I—I needed time to get used to the idea myself," she retorted, annoyed to find she was trembling and that somehow he had put her on the defensive. "And then when I—lost the baby—" She broke off, wetting her dry lips with her tongue, and she saw the convulsive clenching of his hands at his sides. But she could spare no sympathy for him. Whatever regret he was feeling could be nothing compared to the profound sense of loss she had experienced when she miscarried. On top of her broken marriage that final anguish had all but finished her. "There seemed no reason for you to know about the baby —afterward."

"I wouldn't have believed you could be so heartless." He ran one hand around the back of his neck, massaging the muscles there as if they pained him. "I've known all along that you didn't trust me. Now it seems I had reason to distrust you, as well. You had no right to keep a thing like that from me. It was my child, too!"

Bitterness rose like bile in her throat. "You betrayed our marriage vows! At—at least I thought you had. And even if I was wrong then, I'm not anymore."

His eyes brooded on her face. "Do you wish to speak of betrayal?" he inquired, his voice harsh and anguished. "It is you who betrayed me, Rhea! You kept the most important news of my life from me. Do you know that I've spent the last four years trying to forget you? And now I find I didn't even know you, for I would never have thought you could be so cruel. I've been trying to forget a woman who never existed, it seems."

Rhea's dismay made her feel too faint to stand. She sank into an armchair and held her forehead in her hand. Thorne watched her silently.

"We should never have married," she said dully, her voice breaking on the final syllable. "A part of me knew it from the first." She paused to take a trembling breath. "It seems the only thing we have left is our ability to wound each other. I'll agree to a divorce on whatever terms you want. We made a mistake, but there is no reason to continue to live with it."

His "Oh, God!" was at once enraged and wretched. "If you've always believed the marriage was such a mistake, why haven't you filed for a divorce yourself before now?"

Rhea bent her head, her black hair falling across her face. The action exposed the dejected curve of her back, and she was conscious of a sense of emptiness as deep as she had known at the loss of her child. She wished Thorne would leave her before she lost all control of her ragged emotions. Perhaps he sensed this, for a moment later she heard the bedroom door closing, and when she looked up she was alone in front of the fire.

She awoke the next morning before Thorne and left the couch to dress warmly and leave the cabin for a walk. She knew that she would have to face him eventually, but perhaps the cold would be bracing—to her resolve as well as to her constitution. At least it should help to clear the fuzziness from her brain, the result, no doubt, of too little sleep. Thorne's final question of the night before had rung in her head, as if to mock her, long after he had left her. It wasn't that she didn't know the answer, but that she knew it too well.

She had not filed for a divorce because she still loved him. He had seduced her, married her out of a sense of obligation, and then violated the belief she had had in him—and still she loved him. She had told herself that she delayed filing for a divorce because she wanted to avoid the publicity. It had taken Thorne's reappearance to force her to face the deeper reason.

Ironically, now that she had admitted to herself that her feelings for him were unchanged, her acceptance of the necessity of a divorce had an urgency it hadn't had before. A woman could be hurt by the man she loved in ways nobody else could approach. And she couldn't hope to get over him until her last link to him was severed once and for all.

She should feel thankful that Thorne had come back so that divorce proceedings could be set in motion without further delay. Only she didn't. Perhaps this could be explained by the same streak of perversity that had wanted him to make love to her last night.

Sunk in such unhappy thoughts, she had been unconsciously following the tracks left in the snow by Jake Sinclair's tractor. Now she realized that she had covered half the distance to the Sinclairs' cabin and, still unwilling to return to her own place, decided to complete the distance and look in on her neighbors. When she was still several hundred yards away, she saw Jake shoveling snow from the path that led from the road to his front steps.

A few moments later he saw her, too, and waved a welcome, then leaned on his shovel handle to watch her slow progress through the snow.

"Go on in. Maggie's in the kitchen. I want to finish this chore while I'm at it."

Maggie, a short, thin birdlike woman of about sixty whose supply of bustling energy seemed unlimited, peered through the door glass as Rhea was stamping the snow from her boots on the porch.

The door swung open. "This is neighborliness beyond the call of duty," Maggie exclaimed as she wiped flour-dusty hands on a white apron. "Imagine walking so far in this weather!" She hugged Rhea as she stepped into the kitchen. "It's wonderful to see you! Take off your coat and I'll brew a pot of tea."

Rhea deposited coat, scarf, and gloves on a rack near the large wood-burning stove and sat down at the breakfast bar that separated the kitchen from the dining area. As Maggie prepared their tea, she kept up a running commentary on the weather and neighborhood activities, requiring little response from Rhea. However, when the older woman had poured the tea and joined Rhea at the bar, she said suddenly, "You look a bit strained, Rhea. Are you troubled about something?"

Rhea's impulse was to prevaricate, but Maggie's concerned hazel eyes fanned by tiny wrinkles of age and wisdom made her discard the notion. "I guess I am, Maggie. But do you know anyone who hasn't known a bit of trouble now and then?"

Maggie stirred sugar into her tea and said, "Well, it must have something to do with Thorne. Jake told me he was back. The reconciliation isn't working out, I take it."

Rhea smiled slightly. "There never was a reconciliation. I came to the cabin to get away from him when I learned he was in Oklahoma City. Oh, and I want to thank you and Jake for having everything ready for me. I might have saved us all the trouble, though, since Thorne tracked me down anyway. Seems he's suddenly so anxious to start our divorce that he couldn't wait a few days until I returned to the city."

Maggie's look was doubtful. "Is that what he told you?"

"Not exactly." Rhea savored the spicy tang of the hot tea for a moment. "He hasn't had a chance, really. He was so exhausted when he arrived that he went straight to bed. And when he awoke he had a fever. He's been ill ever since."

"Poor man," murmured Maggie with a sympathetic frown. "Is it serious?"

"No. He's had flu or a virus, and he's better now."

"And he still hasn't mentioned divorce?" Maggie's thin, white brows rose questioningly. "Doesn't sound like he's in such an all-fired hurry to me."

"But he didn't deny that it was the purpose for his all-night drive down here when I brought it up."

Maggie looked reflective. "If you're expecting him to beg, Rhea, you mustn't. It isn't in the nature of a man—not any man worth his salt."

"Oh, Maggie, I don't expect anything from Thorne except to be left in peace. He—he's using our situation to make things as difficult for me as possible. He keeps throwing things up to me and—he touches me and—" She stopped, suddenly aware that she was revealing intimacies she never meant to share with anyone.

"So—it's like that, is it?"

"What?"

"It's clear you're still in love with the man."

Maggie's eyes were too discerning for Rhea to attempt an outright denial. Instead, she said, "I'm not sure what I feel at the moment. That's why I was out walking, to try to clear my head. It doesn't seem to have helped. But even if I did love him, it wouldn't change anything. My love for Thorne wasn't enough when we were living together, and it isn't enough now. Oh, Maggie, I think—he's just not like other men."

"Nonsense." Maggie smiled. "Are you sure he's not still in love with you? Maybe he came because he couldn't stay away from you any longer."

Rhea made a bitter sound and forced hot tea past her aching throat. "If you had heard the things he said to me last night, you wouldn't say that. He forced me to tell him about the miscarriage, and then he said I was cruel and heartless, that I'd betrayed him. If he loved me, he couldn't talk to me like that."

"My dear child." Maggie's tone was fondly tolerant. "He was hurt and angry—and to my way of thinking he had some right to be."

Rhea finished her tea then said disconsolately, "You and Jake are determined to take his side, aren't you? Oh, I don't blame you. I know you've always liked Thorne."

"We're mighty partial to you, too. Besides, I'm not taking sides," Maggie denied. "But I still stand by what I said. That baby was Thorne's, too, and you never even told him about it."

Thorne had said the same thing, and hearing it from Maggie's lips made her feel more depressed. She had always sensed an earthy wisdom in Maggie, and it disappointed Rhea to realize that at least part of the older woman's sympathies lay with Thorne.

Back at the cabin Thorne was making scrambled eggs and toast. "You're just in time," he observed as she returned from hanging her coat in the bedroom closet. The food was on the table, and smelling it, Rhea discovered that she was quite hungry. They ate for several moments in awkward silence.

Then Thorne said, "You were up early."

"I felt like a walk, so I went up to the Sinclairs."

"How are they?"

"Well, and seemingly as content as ever. They're very good for each other."

"Yes." After another silence, he said, "I thought I'd try to work this morning, if you've no objections."

She shrugged, wondering what he would say if she did object. But the fact was, she was glad he felt well enough

140

to write. At least he would be too occupied to spare any notice for her. "I'll clean up the kitchen so you can get right to work," she offered.

A few minutes later he'd changed to jeans and a sweater and was sitting in front of the fire, a bulging folder beside him, a yellow legal pad on his knee. The pencil in his hand moved rapidly across the page and he was deep in the world of his imagination. Rhea did the necessary house chores, then curled up in one of the armchairs with a novel. In midafternoon she heated the remainder of the stew and cobbler from the day before and served Thorne's meal on a tray. He ate absentmindedly, his attention still on his writing, and continued to work until the darkness of winter dusk had enclosed the cabin. Rhea, her book fallen aside, was drowsing in the armchair when Thorne spoke.

"Why don't you go to bed? I'll take the couch tonight."

She sat up abruptly, shaking her head, and retrieved her book. "It's too early yet. I'd lie awake for hours."

"Would you like to read some of my manuscript? I have the first couple of chapters in pretty good order."

Rhea, having discovered that the book she had brought with her moved too slowly to hold her interest, accepted the offer with alacrity. "Before I start reading, maybe I should fix something for dinner."

"I'm not hungry," Thorne said. "We had a late lunch. A cup of hot chocolate would be welcome, though."

Rhea made chocolate for both of them and then began reading the manuscript. Before she had reached the end of the first chapter, she realized the book, full of profound and moving understanding of the human condition, was the best thing Thorne had ever written. It was a book no very young man could have written, and she understood now why he had told her four years earlier that he wasn't

141

ready to write it yet. It revealed an author who had experienced his share of joys and tragedies and learned from them.

Later before going to bed, Rhea tried to tell him how touched she had been by what she had read. He listened with clear interest but did not seem inclined to talk about it, and she remembered that he had always been reluctant to discuss a book while he was working on it, claiming that talking dispersed some of the creative energy that should go into the writing.

The next morning Thorne, who always rose early when he was writing, again had breakfast ready when she emerged from the bedroom. "I could get used to this," she quipped without thinking and was rewarded with an ironically crooked smile.

When they had eaten, he announced, "I need some exercise before I get back to the book. How about a walk?"

He seemed completely recovered from his illness, although there was still some gauntness in his face; consequently, Rhea stifled a protest that she realized would have made her sound like a fussy mother—or a dutiful wife! She welcomed the chance to get outside for a bit, too, and they bundled up and left the cabin.

They trudged along in silence for some moments until Thorne's deep voice interrupted her musing. "You're very quiet."

"I was thinking about your book," she told him, blinking against the brilliance of the snow. "The young Choctaw girl, Betsy, is appealing." She spoke haltingly, for as she had read the manuscript the evening before, she had had the impression that the girl Betsy might actually be based on Rhea herself. "The hero is falling in love with her, isn't he?"

"Yes," Thorne replied shortly.

"What will become of Betsy and her lover in the end?"

Thorne glanced down at her with an odd look. "I don't know yet." he said enigmatically. She should have remembered that he never knew the ending of a book when he began it, for he had always said the characters had to tell their own story. Yet there was something significant in his expression that Rhea did not care to examine, so she quickly dropped the subject.

"I need this—" Thorne said after a moment, indicating the forested landscape, "to write the book. Listen and you can almost hear our ancestors moving deep in the woods. Can't you?"

Rhea nodded and smiled up at him. How likable he could be in one of his frivolous moods. She had almost forgotten. It was easy to enter into his imagination with him when he was like this. Suddenly somewhere behind them a branch cracked from the weight of the snow and tumbled to earth.

"That must be your great-great-grandfather out hunting game for his dinner." He bent down and scooped up a handful of snow in his leather glove. "In the old days the Choctaws probably didn't appreciate the beauty of the snow as much as we do since it made hunting and fishing difficult and unpleasant." A strand of Rhea's dark hair had escaped her hood and she brushed it back absentmindedly.

"Do you think they had snowball fights?" Thorne inquired, grinning at her, and she laughed.

His gloved hand closed over the snow, packing it together, and Rhea yelped as it splattered across the front of her coat. She brushed herself off. "If they were anything like you—" But she faltered, her hands growing still as she realized that he was watching her intently.

143

His eyes remained fixed on her face. "I had forgotten what a delightful laugh you have," he said quietly. "I used to tease you just to hear you laugh like that." They stood staring at each other for several seconds until Rhea gave an awkward little smile and turned away to resume walking.

But there was a strain between them. The snow, the isolation, Thorne walking beside her—they only served to lend an air of unreality to the occasion. An observer, had there been one, would have found the scene Christmas-card perfect—too perfect. Rhea felt cut off from the world and time, as if there were no tomorrow. *Maybe there won't be,* she thought sadly, and she could almost wish it were true, a train of thought fraught with perils.

She felt a lump in her throat and peered down at the snow through misty eyes. Oh, God, this was going to be harder than she had ever imagined. Now that he was feeling well again, why hadn't Thorne broached the reason for his arrival—the divorce? Was he waiting for her to bring it up again?

Beside her Thorne began to whistle softly, the cheery sound shocking Rhea into blinking and throwing him a wary look. Maybe he was only trying to break the tension between them.

And then, without warning, he scooped up another handful of snow and turned to splatter her with it. He was laughing lustily, his breath drifting in a white mist up to the snow-laden branches.

It was impossible not to catch some of his spirit. "Devil!" Rhea shrieked and bent to clutch a handful of snow for retaliation. And suddenly they were like two children, dodging between the trees, pelting each other with snowballs. Thorne's aim was more accurate, however, and soon Rhea's hood had fallen back and her hair and coat were snow-frosted and she was laughing helplessly. Then, as another snowball landed on her shoulder, she stepped backwards and fell flat in a snowdrift.

Now Thorne had fallen beside her, and they tumbled deeper into the drift, out of breath from laughing. And then she grew still as Thorne loomed darkly above her. His strong hands brushed the snow from her hair, but he was no longer laughing and Rhea had a sudden feeling that they were both holding their breath.

Snow glistened in his black hair, and she wanted to spread her fingers through it. She felt as if she were falling as he drew her against him. "I have you at my mercy now," he whispered, only half teasing, kissing her lips, the hollows of her eyes. "Do you recognize this place?"

She looked about and saw the hackberry tree where she'd had her treehouse as a child. Thorne's knowing look told her he was recalling the first time they had made love—here beneath the hackberry. It had been summer—the woods green and verdant, the grass soft and the sunlight warm to their naked bodies . . .

"You do remember, don't you?" he said with a half smile. "It's not so enticing with snow on the ground. Don't you think we'd be more comfortable inside?"

Rhea swallowed hard and stared at him. "No," she managed to say. "Last night things got out of hand. I won't let it happen again."

"You don't really mean that," Thorne chided. "After all, we're stuck here together for another few days. We might as well enjoy it." He gazed down at her. "I've been wondering if you didn't come here hoping I would follow. If so, it was a lovely idea."

Rhea resented his words as well as his casual assumption that she was there for his pleasure. Had she not been, any other woman would have done as well. Rhea felt hurt and tears sprang to her eyes, but she forced them back and pushed him roughly away.

"If I had been interested in a romantic interlude," she said deliberately, "I could have had it in Oklahoma City."

His face went rigid and she knew he had assumed she referred to Don Cragmont. Well, let him. If the idea that some other man might be attractive to her wounded his pride, he deserved it.

"Where are you going?" Thorne stormed as she scrambled to her feet.

"Back to the cabin." She brushed some of the snow from her coat and pushed past him, her one glance taking in his face drawn with anger, and she fled.

"Rhea!"

But she didn't look back. It was ten minutes or so before Thorne followed her. The look on his face told her he was still angry. When she plopped into a chair and tried to pretend an interest in a magazine, he lifted it from her hands and tossed it onto the couch.

"I want to talk to you." He had removed his outer clothing and stood towering over her chair, his legs in the tightly clinging jeans spread, his sweatered arms crossed in front of him. "Clare Rutledge told me that you have been seeing Cragmont regularly for a good while."

His peremptory tone infuriated her. "Goodness, Clare was a fountain of information, wasn't she?"

"Are you in love with him?"

Bristling even more, Rhea retorted, "What right have you to ask me that? I have dated only one man since our separation and you've been with dozens of women!"

His jaw clenched. "The fact that there were dozens should tell you none of them meant anything to me."

"Oh, well—" she flared, "that makes it all right, doesn't it?"

He caught hold of her wrists and jerked her to her feet. "Damn you!" he hissed. "Are you in love with Cragmont? Answer me!"

"I will not!" Her eyes flashed defiantly. "And I won't listen to a word against Don, either. He has always been kind to me."

"I'm sure," sneered Thorne savagely, his lean face taut with anger. "Well, you listen to me, Rhea. You had better wait until you're out of one marriage before you contemplate another one."

"*What!*" How dare he assume that authoritative tone with her. "You—you can't tell me what to contemplate!"

"You are still my wife," he retorted, losing color with a suddenness that left him pale and gaunt.

"There is nothing but a legal technicality between us."

His expression grew dark as he glared at her, and Rhea wrenched free of his hands. He regarded her solemnly, his dark eyes rapidly losing all expression.

"So—" he uttered between stiff lips. "There is nothing between us, eh? Yet we both know that I can still arouse you. There has to be some feeling left."

"No."

His eyes glittered like chips of black ice. "Sexual attraction then, if I must be blunt. But perhaps you find Cragmont more to your liking."

Rhea's lips moved stiffly. "That's really all you want from a woman, isn't it, Thorne? And since you have decided to bury yourself in the woods, women aren't quite as available to you as they have been in the past. Such an inconvenience! So you think you can use me!"

She spoke harshly and angrily, venting all her pent-up frustration and emotion in a rush of cruel words, hardly aware of the effect they were having on Thorne. But he took one threatening step toward her and she realized how furious he was. She fell back against the chair and he, exercising an immense effort of will, stood still, glaring at her.

Then he looked away, raking his fingers through his damp hair. "Oh, damnation!" he grated. And he strode into the bedroom and slammed the door behind him.

Chapter 8

It was two days later when Maggie and Jake arrived on their tractor for an afternoon visit. Rhea had never been so glad to see anyone in her life. Since her confrontation with Thorne after their walk in the snow, they had given each other a wide berth, speaking only when necessary and then with great restraint and careful politeness. Thorne had passed the time writing, but Rhea had no such occupation in which she could lose herself for hours at a stretch.

"We had cabin fever," Maggie announced as she and Jake came through the door. "So we decided to barge in on you two. I brought some fresh-baked cookies." She handed a foil-wrapped parcel to Rhea.

"I'm glad you came," Rhea assured the two of them. She glanced briefly at Thorne, who had risen from his seat on the couch. "We can certainly use some company."

While Thorne exchanged greetings with the Sinclairs, she made coffee and arranged Maggie's chocolate-chip cookies on a plate, which she brought to the others in front of the fire. She took one of the armchairs and settled back to listen as Maggie and Jake questioned Thorne about his work and his plans for the future.

"I'm back in Oklahoma to stay," he told them, effectively putting to rest any doubts Rhea might have had about the finality of that decision.

"Here?" Jake inquired. "Or will you be staying in Poteau with your sister?"

Rhea stared into her coffee as Thorne responded. "I haven't made final arrangements yet, although I'm sure I won't be staying with Gracie. I'll be getting a place of my own."

"Oh . . ." Jake looked over at Rhea, evidently feeling he had stuck his foot in his mouth. "Well—uh—you're working on a new book, are you? I hope we didn't come at a bad time. We thought you and Rhea might be feeling a bit restless, too, and enjoy a game of cards. But if you're working, Thorne . . ."

"I could use a break," Thorne said. He looked at Rhea. "Do you have a deck around?"

Maggie reached into the pocket of her heavy sweater. "We brought one with us."

Thorne laughed. "I see you're just as efficient as I remember, Maggie," and the white-haired woman flushed prettily.

They moved to the kitchen table and spent the next couple of hours playing pitch. Maggie and Rhea teamed as partners against the men. The Sinclairs' fond teasing of each other as the game progressed dispelled the tension that had lain heavily upon the cabin before their arrival, and Rhea found herself relaxing for the first time in days.

Jake's face was screwed up as he contemplated his cards and Maggie chided, "Don't do anything rash, dearie. We set you good the last time you bid."

To which Jake replied, "Crow while you can, Maggie, my girl, for Thorne and I are about to make a comeback. I believe I'll just bid four on this little hand."

"Four!" chortled Maggie. She winked at Rhea. "He always gets desperate when he's losing."

"You can see she's not used to winning," Jake came back. "She doesn't know how to handle it with any grace at all."

The Sinclairs were so good together, Rhea thought, so comfortable and content. As Jake played his ace, she let herself wish fleetingly that she and Thorne could have known the kind of relationship the Sinclairs had. It was her turn to play, and she flicked that errant thought aside quickly as she laid her card on the table.

She dreaded the time when the Sinclairs would leave her and Thorne alone again. Her dread, of course, only made the time fly faster until Jake said, "If we'd had time for another couple of hands, we'd have beaten you two gals. But if we don't leave now it'll be dark before we get home."

Maggie gave him an arch look. "Excuses, excuses."

"Seems we'll have to give them a rematch," Jake said. "Can't let women get too uppity. Right, Thorne?"

"Right," Thorne agreed, slanting a wry glance in Rhea's direction.

The Sinclairs got into their coats, issuing invitations for Thorne and Rhea to come up to their cabin for a visit any time. And then they were gone, the sound of their tractor roaring to life outside.

Rhea ran water into the sink to wash the coffee cups—anything to shatter the uneasy silence left by the Sinclairs' departure. After depositing the cups in the draining rack, she turned to find Thorne still standing in the kitchen entrance, watching her.

Her heart missed a beat as Thorne's eyes probed her face. "Do you have any alcohol around?"

"There's a bottle of wine at the back of the corner cabinet. Will that do?"

"It'll have to," he said in an even tone. He moved past her to the cabinet. She turned to watch him getting a glass, pouring the wine. "Want some?" he inquired, his back to her. His shoulders were slumped, as if he had been exerting a false cheer for the Sinclairs' benefit, and now that they were gone he was tired from the masquerade.

"No."

He turned to look at her, glass in hand, his expression tightly under control, as though he were having trouble holding himself back from some bitter vituperation.

"I—I'm sorry there's nothing stronger. I know you're used to—"

That had been the wrong thing to say, she realized at once. His strong features were taut, the wide mouth straight and unsmiling. "I haven't had a drop in months, ever since I discovered it wasn't an answer—to anything." He sauntered to the couch and flung himself down, the glass in his hand. Sipping the wine, he surveyed her from beneath dark brows. Rhea felt her nerves quiver.

She knew they could not go on like this, wondered wildly when the wrecker service Jake had contacted would get through to them. She knew an almost overwhelming urge to escape, but outside darkness was already creeping stealthily through the trees, closing them in. Why was he looking at her like that? What did he want? Why couldn't he have stayed in Oklahoma City and let her have the time to gather her composure, to steel herself for their meeting?

She actually felt that she might go mad if it wasn't over soon. How could she begin to put Thorne and what had been between them behind her as long as they were in the cabin together? If only they had gotten the divorce four years ago . . .

"What are you thinking?" he demanded.

"I was thinking about—our situation."

"And what conclusions have you reached?"

She walked slowly to a chair next to the fire and sat down, straight-backed, meeting his look with difficulty. She knew what had to be said, but oddly it was extremely difficult to say it. Still, to have things settled between them would be better than this tense waiting.

She took a deep breath. "I know this hasn't been easy for you, either. It's been an unfortunate set of circumstances for both of us."

His mouth quirked sardonically. "What do you propose we do about it?"

"There is only one thing to do, isn't there? We both need a fresh start. We have to start divorce proceedings as soon as we get out of here. If—if you don't want to take time from your work, I'll see a lawyer and start whatever has to be done."

He swallowed the remaining wine in his glass in one gulp and, incredibly, she got the feeling that he was nervous and using the drink to steady himself. She gave herself a mental shake. What an unlikely idea! Thorne wanted a divorce as much as she did. In fact, he had wanted it so much that he couldn't even wait until she returned to Oklahoma City to discuss it.

"We never gave our marriage much of a chance," he said suddenly, staring into his empty glass. "If Cragmont hadn't been on hand when you were so vulnerable—"

"Don has nothing to do with the failure of our marriage," she said wearily.

He gave a sigh. "Sorry, but I can't accept that." He twirled his glass idly, staring into the fire as if trying to decide what to say next. Finally he went on tautly, "I hate the idea of letting him move in on you after our divorce."

"You haven't anything to say about what I do once I'm free!"

"I know that intellectually," he said coolly, "but that doesn't stop me feeling that I have, or ought to have."

She remembered suddenly a Hollywood starlet who had, according to the scandal sheets, tried to drown herself in a swimming pool after Thorne dropped her. Did he think that Rhea might do something equally as foolish?

She lifted her head in a gesture of courage. "You needn't feel in any way responsible for me," she said huskily. "My experience with marriage hasn't exactly endeared the institution to me, so don't think I'll go into another one without giving it long and careful thought." She felt something tighten in her throat, and getting up, she walked to the window, her hand gripping the edge of the curtain.

"So," she muttered, wishing she could stop the trembling that was running through her limbs. "I'll see a lawyer as soon as I get back to the city."

When he did not answer, she turned to look across the room at him. He had risen from the couch and was standing, his arms crossed over his chest, watching her, and the look in his dark eyes made her heart thud frighteningly.

"Very well," he said finally. Then he got his coat, put it on, and went to the front door. "I'm going for a walk."

She understood his need to get away from her. She would have liked to go out, too—in another direction from Thorne's. But it was dark and cold, so instead she went in to shower and get into her night clothes before Thorne's return. Then, even though it was quite early, she turned out the bedroom light and got into bed. She wasn't hungry, and if Thorne wanted dinner he would have to fix it himself.

She stared bleakly into the shadows of the room until, some time later, she heard Thorne return. She turned on her side, her face to the wall, and feigned sleep while he showered and moved quietly about the room, finally closing the bedroom door behind him.

It must have been after midnight when she stopped tossing and turning and fell into a fitful sleep. And it could have been little more than two hours later that she came awake with a start, having dreamt that she was on top of a snow-covered mountain and, having lost her footing, had begun to slide with dangerous speed down the sheer drop to the valley far below. She had looked back and saw Thorne standing atop the mountain, although before she had been alone. She cried out desperately for him to save her, but he merely stood there and watched her fall.

Sighing with a profound weariness, she threw back the covers, slipping her feet into scuffs as she got out of bed. She put on her robe and opened the bedroom door carefully, intending to go quietly into the kitchen and make a cup of chocolate to take back to bed with her. Perhaps it would help her relax enough to sleep.

He had left a table lamp on, and he was stretched out on the couch in his tan robe, one long arm flung across his face. He stirred as she moved across the room and sat up with a groan.

Rhea halted to say apologetically, "I'm sorry. I didn't mean to wake you."

He ran both hands over his face. "It's all right. I wasn't asleep." The words were muffled by his hands. "I was writing until a little while ago." He took his hands away and lifted his head to look at her. "What are you doing?"

"I can't sleep. I shouldn't have gone to bed so early. I thought I'd make a cup of chocolate."

"Make two, will you?"

While she made the chocolate, he stirred the dying fire and placed logs over the red embers. When she brought his mug, he took it and, when she started to go back to the bedroom, said, "You might as well sit here by the fire. You don't look as if you'll sleep soon, and I'm certain I won't."

She knew it was ridiculous to try to avoid him for the remainder of their time together, and she was already bone-sore from twisting about on the bed. So she sat down on the stone hearth to get the most benefit from the flames that were beginning to lick upward around the logs Thorne had laid.

He didn't seem angry anymore, merely tired. "You never used to work so late," she said, thinking that he appeared somehow driven. Perhaps he felt a sense of urgency to finish the book, or perhaps the book was a release from whatever was driving him. In either case it seemed unlikely he could stand up for very long under such a rigorous regime as he had set for himself the last few days. "You always told me you couldn't be creative for longer than four or five hours at a stretch."

"There's some truth in that," he said, "but, also, when we were together, I wanted to spend as much time with you as I could. I used to find it difficult to write for even four hours, knowing you were in the apartment. Were you aware of that?"

She shook her head, not knowing what to say.

"Well, it's true."

She lowered her lashes and said defensively, "Then it seems your work should have improved when I left."

Her tone was deliberately offhand. She did not want to

give Thorne the idea that she felt in any way responsible for the fact that his recent novels lacked the depth of the earlier ones.

He drew breath harshly. "On the contrary. I couldn't work at all for a good while. I wasn't much use for anything but to wonder what I had done or left undone that made you leave as you did. It seemed the height of audacity even to think of writing novels that delved into the innermost secrets of human hearts when I couldn't even figure out my own wife." In the silence that followed this bitter revelation, Rhea heard her heart pounding.

"I'm sorry," Thorne went on after a moment. "I've no right to lay all that on you. I'm sorry, too, that I blundered in here like a bellowing bull moose. I didn't know I wouldn't be able to leave whenever I wanted, but I should have respected your clear wish to avoid me."

"No—don't apologize. We had to see each other sometime. At least, we—understand each other a little better now."

"Do we?" There was irony in the question. He was watching her with an expression that seemed uncertain. He took a swallow of his chocolate, holding the cup firmly in both hands. When he lowered it, he asked in a musing tone, "Were you glad when you lost the baby?"

Rhea couldn't say anything for a moment. She just put down her chocolate and stared at him. "No—and I resent your even thinking it, Thorne."

He shrugged. "I merely assumed—"

"Why would you assume that losing my baby would make me happy? Do you see me as such an unnatural woman?"

"No—only if you'd had the baby you'd have had a perpetual reminder of me around."

Good Lord, did he think she needed a baby for *that*

—when a faintly heard melody, the set of a man's shoulders ahead of her in a crowd, an idle phrase spoken by a stranger could remind her of him? Once she knew she was pregnant, she had wanted the baby so that she would have a part of Thorne with her always.

"I wanted the baby, Thorne. I had a difficult time after the miscarriage. So much so that I saw a psychologist for several weeks. He helped me deal with the loss."

He got up and came to stand over her, frowning. "I should have been the one to do that. If only you had let me know. If you had believed in me even a little . . ."

Rhea made a helpless gesture. "We've been over that already. You were getting ready to go to California and, besides, there was no point."

His hand on her shoulder forced her to look up at him. "I want to tell you something, not that it's going to change anything now. I'd just like to clear the air." He pulled her to her feet. "I didn't track you down to talk about a divorce."

Her bewildered eyes rose to his hard face. "Then why—?"

"I had a stupidly misguided notion," he said, the words seeming to mock himself, "that we might be able to try again together. Unrealistic of me, wasn't it? I didn't think about how four years can change people. I guess it was finding out about the miscarriage that forced me to accept the fact that you really want nothing to do with me, that you aren't willing to trust me again. When people don't trust each other, there isn't much to build a marriage on, is there?"

She shook her head, distressed. "No . . . I'm sorry . . ."

His lids dropped, hiding his eyes, and he made a contemptuous sound. "I guess that's the real indication of a finished marriage—when two people keep apologizing to each other, as if they were polite strangers."

Rhea's face was burning, her eyes pained. "I'm sorry . . ."

"Oh, hell, stop apologizing!" His eyes lifted to flick over her face and the low V of her robe. "You are still," he muttered, as if the admission disgusted him, "the most desirable woman I ever knew." His fingers came up to touch her cheek and run through the silken fall of her hair. "Do you know I often dream of waking up to find you in my bed with your hair streaming across my shoulder?"

Rhea's breath caught. She could not look away from him. Dear God, how she wanted him! Would this weakness torture her for the rest of her life? She looked at his mouth, her heart throbbing. It came nearer—or perhaps she only imagined that it did because suddenly she wanted it so desperately—and with a sucked-in breath she lifted her face to him.

Thorne gave a stifled sound of hunger, then his mouth grazed her cheek and found her lips opened like the petals of a flower welcoming the probing of a honey bee.

Her body trembled in his arms, her eyes closed, her hands moved clutchingly over his shoulders, the rough touch of his sweater under her palms. She kissed him with a desperation she could not disguise and knew a triumphant sense of power as he deepened the kiss, bruising her soft lips and sending fire leaping along her veins.

Then panic intruded. Could she actually be doing this? After they had agreed to start divorce proceedings immediately, how could she be so bereft of pride as to offer herself to him? But she wanted him so badly. Could one more time matter that much? Her brain still awhirl with confusion, she realized that Thorne had lifted his head and was breathing raggedly.

"I don't want this . . ."

Rhea stared at him, hating the bitter expression on his face. Her stomach clenched in a painful knot. She felt her lips tighten. "I didn't mean to push myself on you," she said unsteadily. "Forgive me." Oh, Lord, was she going to spend the next few days apologizing for not trusting him—for wanting him—perhaps even for breathing?

She stumbled away from him, half running from the room. In bed, she pulled the covers up over her shaking body. She didn't understand anything. He had said that he found her desirable—and then he had turned her down when she offered herself. Oh, God, the knowledge humiliated, but that *is* what she had done. Had he deliberately led her on so that he could reject her? To get his own back—because she hadn't told him about the baby? Could he be that coldly calculating?

I don't want this . . . The words burned in her brain. Thank God she hadn't told him that she still loved him, even though the admission had trembled at the back of her throat for a brief moment. Thank God she hadn't lowered herself that far.

But it was small consolation.

Chapter 9

Sleep was impossible. She tossed and turned in real desperation. This was what came of loving one man so hopelessly, she thought, swallowing the bitter taste in her mouth. The expression "a one-man woman" had always struck her as being overly romantic and unrealistic. Lately she had even started to convince herself that the fondness she felt for Don Cragmont could, given enough time, grow into love, love that was quiet and undemanding, free of the dangerously explosive passions Thorne had unleashed. Seeing Thorne again had knocked that theory into a cocked hat. If there ever was a one-man woman, it was she, and the knowledge was repulsive to her.

Her restless tossing continued until her nerves screamed and she flung her pillow aside and sat up on the side of the bed. Perhaps she should go up to the Sinclairs tomorrow and ask to be allowed to move into their spare room, she thought despairingly. But she had no right to burden them with her problems, and they might see it as a request to take sides with her against Thorne. It wouldn't be fair. . . .

The knock at the bedroom door jolted along her already too tight nerves. "We have to talk." Thorne's voice was as hard as stone.

"*No!*"

"Rhea, I'm coming in . . ."

"There's nothing to talk about!" Her voice was shrill with unreasoning panic. "Just leave me alone!"

She heard his muttered curse as he flung open the door, throwing a shaft of pale lamplight before him to split the room in two. He peered at her, then walked to the window beside her bed to stare out at nothing.

"I want you to understand what happened earlier."

Her breathing was labored. "It is perfectly clear to me. Now get out of my bedroom, Thorne."

He flicked a glance at her, then turned back to the window. "You don't understand anything."

She clutched her head in her hands. "You don't have to draw a diagram for me. You were trying to prove that you could make me—want you, and you did. A woman can be sexually attracted to someone she despises. Do you expect a medal for proving that? You aren't the first person to discover it, you know."

He made a harsh sound deep in his throat. "I was angry because you were offering me your body without love— like so many of the women I have known. Fool that I am, I wanted to believe you were better than that."

"And your sensibilities were offended?" A thready laugh escaped her. "What rubbish! You really enjoy making me feel rotten, don't you?"

He turned to face her. "Why should you feel rotten? I'm the one who's had the props knocked out from under me."

"Because I'm no longer the romantic, ignorant little girl

162

you married? What do you think it does for *my* self-esteem to know that not only is our marriage a miserable failure, but you don't find me even slightly desirable anymore? Oh, I've gotten the message, Thorne, loud and clear."

His hand ran roughly through his rumpled hair. "You know I wanted you," he said, his voice thickened. "I've been lying on the couch torturing myself with visions of you and Don Cragmont. It has even occurred to me that he might not have been the only one. You are a passionate woman."

"Oh, I see." She shivered weakly, although the room was warm. "It's fine for you to behave like a—an alley cat—but it's not acceptable for me to do so?"

"Damn it! No, it isn't acceptable—and don't throw the old double-standard argument in my face. I can't help what I feel."

"You're welcome to your feelings, but don't try to impose them on me. I lost my rose-colored glasses when I saw Diane come out of your bedroom four years ago." She buried her face in her hands, refusing to look at him. Her flesh felt hot, and yet she still trembled.

"Why won't you look at me?" He paused and she forced herself to lift her head. His wide mouth was sensual yet set in merciless lines. "I'm sick of hearing about Diane. I am going to explain something to you again, and you are going to listen carefully. My relationship with Diane was over long before I met you. She had been trying to resume it, but I wanted nothing more to do with her aside from business. That did not change once we were married. I didn't need or want Diane or any other woman. I fully expected to feel that way for the rest of my life." His voice grated fiercely in the quietness. "Diane didn't want to accept that. You must have realized she was the sort of person who finds it difficult to take no for an answer—

163

about anything. It's what makes her so successful as an agent. That little scene she staged—and it was staged, Rhea—was a last-ditch effort to get what she wanted."

"Well, it worked, didn't it?" Rhea inquired.

Thorne's eyes glittered down at her. "No. After you left, I wanted even less to re-establish anything with Diane. Eventually, I decided I didn't even want to continue a business relationship with her and I switched to another agency. I was not unfaithful to you from the day we met until long after you walked out on me."

Rhea's protest was a faint, choking sound. "What does 'long after' mean to you, Thorne? Weeks, a few months? Well, however long it was, you certainly made up for lost time once you'd 'recovered'! I daresay you couldn't even recall the number of women you've had in the past four years if your life depended on it!"

He contemplated her for a long moment, then abruptly he sat down beside her. She was conscious of his breathing, the rise and fall of the muscled chest, the movement of his hand as it touched her shoulder.

Closing her eyes, she tried to slow the sickening speed of her heart. "Don't—don't touch me."

His hand dropped away, but he continued to sit beside her, his body stiffening. "I'm not going to tell you there wasn't a woman or two, but not nearly as many as the scandal sheets implied. You know that most of what's printed in those rags is outright lies. None of them meant anything to me, and the feeling was mutual."

She flicked a derisive look at him. "What about that girl who tried to drown herself?"

"What—?" He frowned, then laughed humorlessly. "Beth something or other? I hardly knew the girl. We danced together a few times at a party. I hadn't even seen her in weeks when she fell into that pool. I was told by a friend of hers that it was accidental. She was intoxicated—with drink or drugs, who knows? The rest was the figment of some muckracking reporter's imagination. Once you are in the public eye, you are fair game."

When she did not respond, he went on raggedly, "As time passed and I never heard from you, I wanted to exorcise you from my memory. I wanted to be able to look at you and feel no desire at all. It became my chief goal in life. I tried work and more work. I tried booze—and women."

"Well, you've succeeded admirably well," she retorted bitterly. "I congratulate you."

"No," he said wearily. "No, I haven't."

Her numbed mind could not take in what he was saying. She looked into his face. Despite everything his tormented look wrung her heart. Against her will she touched the deep lines etched beside his mouth, wanting to erase them. But she was not prepared for his savage response. He grasped her hand, pulling it away from his face. "I've been going crazy imprisoned in this cabin with you, wanting to touch you but never knowing how you would react. Do you enjoy watching me writhe, Rhea?"

For long seconds his eyes bored mercilessly into hers. Then, with a swift movement, he pulled her toward him and his mouth took cruel possession of hers, parting her lips and plundering her mouth with a ruthlessness that took no notice of her feeble struggles to break free.

His mouth left hers to pillage her throat, wreaking havoc on her unraveling emotions. Her head fell back in unconscious invitation. She whimpered, stifled and helpless. His hands moved over her in ravenous hunger, bruising one moment, fondling the next. His fingers seemed to be separate fires, hot embers of a naked desire that com-

165

municated itself to her, mounting to her head and leaving her powerless in his arms.

He pushed her down on the bed, his kisses still working their bittersweet torture on her dazed senses. She was so bemused that she hardly knew when he moved away and she did not open her eyes, wanting to sink farther and farther into the mire of heady sensations. When she felt the mattress sink with his weight again, she opened her eyes and blinked at him as if coming back to reality after a dream-filled sleep. He was naked, his discarded robe a heap on the floor.

Seeing him like that caused heat to pour through her bloodstream. The dim light from the next room bathed his body, giving a bronze sheen to his broad shoulders and the leanly muscled limbs. Her eyes widened and quickly moved away.

She turned away from him, but he cupped her chin with a strong hand and forced her head back. As she stared up at him, paralyzed, hypnotized, his other hand pulled roughly at her gown. He lifted her slightly and easily freed her body of the clinging fabric. Then his hand ran down her and she moaned, making one last feeble movement to leave the bed.

But his arms held her fast. "How beautiful you are," he murmured as he bent his black head to touch the warm roundness of her breast.

"Ah, Rhea . . . Rhea . . . Let me make love to you."

There was a note of pleading in the tone. He had begun a tender seduction, his lips tracing the contours of her breasts and stomach, his fingers gently outlining her hip and thigh.

He lifted his head and looked down into her wide, glazed eyes. She couldn't move and his eyes held hers as he touched her intimately, possessively.

166

The sensual line of his mouth came down to claim hers, and her lips parted to receive his kiss. As the kiss deepened, her arms crept up his chest to encircle his neck. She felt the warm, soothing stroke of his fingertips exploring the secret places of her body.

He released her lips briefly to say in a strange low tone, "In this one way, at least, you belong to me." She could not have stopped the moan of pleasure that escaped her had she tried. He looked at her flushed face, her closed eyes, and uttered a sharp, triumphant groan as he moved over her.

The drumming of her heart seemed to drown out all other sounds. For a brief moment her fevered brain caught at the tail end of reason as it receded in the face of a consuming desire. In that moment she realized what was happening, understood that Thorne had unleashed in her the fevered hunger that she had known with no other man, that he was aware of what he was doing, was doing it deliberately, using all the consummate skill of which he was capable to gain her surrender. But the moment passed as his mouth closed round her breast again and she sank without a struggle into the warm, dark seas of pleasurable sensations.

Once he cried out her name—a sound filled with emotion dredged up from the deepest part of him—and she could not hate him for what he had done. Instead she ran shaking hands over his head, holding him close against her, and moved with him toward the satisfaction they both craved.

Afterward he drifted into sleep, his arms holding her fast against him, her head on his shoulder, their bodies still tangled together.

She lay awake, every nerve and cell of her body filled with him. She thought dazedly that he had branded her with the mark of his possession, insinuated himself through the barrier of her skin to warm the blood in her veins and filter down to bring life to the farthest nerve.

It could never be this way with anyone else. She knew that now. But knowing it did not turn her into the naive young woman she had been when she met Thorne. Nor did it turn him into the sort of man whose need for a woman softened and weakened him.

He would always be stubborn and proud and hot-tempered and all the other things that made Thorne Folsom. He might never fully forgive her for leaving him as she had or for not telling him about the baby.

Even if he loved her as she had once believed he did, he wouldn't change.

After a while she fell asleep and slept deeply. In the morning, as soon as she opened her eyes, she turned her head to one side and found the bed empty beside her. Thorne had gone.

Chapter 10

She took longer than was necessary getting dressed because she was finding it difficult to face Thorne after last night. In the cold dim light of morning, it seemed to her that he had wanted to prove once and for all her vulnerability where he was concerned. He had even said that she belonged to him, as if she were a *thing* to be owned and kept conveniently at hand as long as she proved useful.

Oh, he had admitted that he hadn't managed totally to forget her during their separation; and clearly he was jealous of Don Cragmont. But could a man be held responsible for the things he said while in the throes of physical desire? And never, since his return, had he said that he loved her.

She stood at the closed bedroom door, breathing in the fragrance of burning cedar logs. She knew that Thorne wanted to stay at the cabin while he finished his book. Did he also fancy the convenience of a weekend wife during his self-imposed exile in the woods? Were these his motives in making love to her last night?

Thorne was sitting in front of the fire, his writing pad on his knee, when she entered the living room. When he looked up, his abstracted expression made her feel that she was intruding. Which was ridiculous. It was *her* cabin.

For a moment there was also a hint of wariness, of waiting, in his dark eyes. But he spoke carelessly. "Good morning, Rhea. I hope you slept well."

"Well enough," she admitted grudgingly.

"There's coffee on the stove."

She poured herself a cup, thinking that he was evidently no longer trying to impress her with his domesticity since he hadn't made breakfast. Perhaps he felt he had her where he wanted her already? Well, she didn't feel like eating breakfast, anyway, but it seemed important to repudiate any assumptions Thorne might have made because of last night.

She finished the coffee before she spoke. "I'm going up to the Sinclairs."

He laid aside his pad and regarded her uncertainly. "Why?"

"I—I want to call the office. I should let Don know that I'm snowed in here and that I probably won't be back to work for another few days."

"Are you going to tell him about last night?"

She felt heat running up her face. Her brown eyes flared with anger. "Of course not!"

He laughed unpleasantly. "Why? Because you don't want him to know how cozy we've become, or because it's not important to you?"

He was affronted because she could go on with organizing her life as if he hadn't barged back into it again. He wanted her to be shattered, to be concerned only with him and his needs, as his other women no doubt had been.

Calling on all her reserves of strength, she met his insolent gaze, her dark eyes steady under the black arch of her brows. "Last night didn't really change anything, Thorne. All problems can't be solved in bed."

"Oh? That sounds like the voice of experience." His tone had gone stone-cold, but his eyes blazed. "What do you and Cragmont use instead of the bed? Perhaps I can discover where I went wrong." She saw the anger in him, although he was keeping it very much contained, his eyes half shielded by his lids, his jaw muscles tight.

She did not answer but went into the bedroom to put on her coat. When she returned to the living room, Thorne hadn't taken up his pad again but was sitting sprawled in his chair, his hands locked behind his head. "Give Jake and Maggie my regards," he said.

"All right," she replied as she went out the door. She stood for a moment on the porch, pulling on her gloves and trying to fathom the odd finality she had heard in Thorne's last statement.

She looked down at her booted feet as she left the porch and headed up the tractor trail in the direction of the Sinclairs' cabin. The ache that had been lying dully in her since awaking seemed to grow heavier as she trudged along. Why was love so painful? Why couldn't it always be the hearts and flowers the poets wrote about?

The temperature was higher than it had been since her arrival, and the packed snow beneath her boots was becoming slushy around the edges of the tire marks. Even the snow on either side of the trail that hadn't been disturbed was losing its pure whiteness and was taking on a gray tinge. Or was she seeing her surroundings through a gray veil of unhappiness?

As she walked, pride and love warred inside her. Was it possible that Thorne might still be willing to try to salvage their marriage? But how could she ever again feel sure of him? Was she expected to make all the concessions? How did she know he wouldn't turn to someone else if things didn't work out as he wanted? She couldn't take another betrayal. Maybe it was better to suffer the sharp pain of a clean break than to lay herself open to the rending anguish that could go on for years if she abandoned wisdom and followed where her emotions led. She had done that once, and look where it had landed her.

She was still no closer to an answer when Maggie and Jake's cabin came into view, a warm trail of wood smoke rising from the chimney. She hurried the last several yards to the porch and ran up the front steps.

She heard footsteps inside and then Maggie answered her knock. "Rhea! I was just thinking about you. Where's Thorne?"

"He didn't come. I'd like to use your telephone."

Maggie took her coat and gloves and carried them to the old-fashioned rack in a corner near the fire. Then she put on water for tea while Rhea made her call on the kitchen wall phone, reversing the charges. Don had just walked into his office and sounded breathless as he came on the line, as if he'd been running.

"I expected to hear from you before this," he told her bluntly.

"I don't have a phone in my cabin. I'm calling from a neighbor's."

"When are you coming back to work?"

"In two or three days. My car's in a ditch, but the neighbor phoned a wrecker for me. It should be out here before too much longer. The roads have been awful."

"It can't be too soon for me," he told her, an edge of harried irritation in his tone. "The girl they sent over from the temporary office help agency can type reasonably well, but she knows nothing about archival work. Clare or I

172

have to tell her every step to take. There's going to be a lot of work waiting for you when you get back. Oh, and speaking of Clare, there's something you should know. Thorne called here the day you left, demanding to know where you were and when you'd be back. He didn't get anything from me, but he waylaid Clare after work and invited her to dinner. She didn't know you wanted to avoid him, so she may have given away your hiding place. When I told her what she'd done, she felt really bad about it."

"Don." Rhea finally managed to cut into his monologue. "I know all that. Thorne came to the cabin."

There was a moment of silence on the other end of the wire. Then, "He's got a nerve! What happened? I suppose he forced his way in."

"No, he didn't. There was little point in refusing him entrance after he'd come all this way to talk to me. Anyway, tell Clare I don't blame her. I know how persuasive Thorne can be. She probably didn't even realize she was giving anything away."

"He can be persuasive, can he?" Don's voice sounded suspicious. "Has he been trying to persuade you?"

"I don't know what you mean," Rhea retorted brightly.

"Does he want a divorce?"

"We—we talked about that, yes."

He must have caught the unconscious hesitation in her words. "What's wrong?" he asked in a low voice.

"Nothing." Rhea managed to inject some conviction into the reply. "I'm getting restless, being stranded here. It shouldn't go on for much longer, though. Say hello to everyone. I'd better hang up now. Good-bye, Don."

"Rhea, wait!"

Her hand, holding the receiver, was already poised over the wall receptacle and she pretended not to hear his plea as she dropped it into place. She stared at the phone for a moment before turning to face Maggie.

"You've been frowning like that every time I've seen you this week," Maggie commented, eyeing her austerely. "Didn't anybody ever tell you frowning will age you before your time?"

Rubbing at the lines between her brows with her fingertips, Rhea heard herself laugh and winced at the false sound of it.

"Let's go in by the fire," Maggie suggested as she lifted the tea tray. Rhea followed the other woman's slight figure into the living room and, as Maggie set the tea things on a low coffee table, sat down on the couch. After pouring their tea, Maggie sat beside her.

"Ummm, I needed this," Rhea said. She glanced toward the door leading into the hallway. "Where's Jake?"

"In his workshop repairing a kitchen chair. He'll be busy out there most of the morning." Maggie gave Rhea a troubled look. "Tea's not going to fix what's ailing you, honey. You and Thorne aren't hitting it off at all, are you?"

"Maggie," she retorted, her voice sounding too shrill to belong to her, "that is putting it mildly."

Maggie had perplexity in her eyes. "I can't believe that with enough love two grown people can't solve their differences."

"Love," she said on a sharp note, "doesn't work so well when it's one-sided. Oh, I'm sick of it, Maggie! I'm tired of being used, of being expected to settle for Thorne's crumbs and—"

Staring at her, Maggie said bewilderedly, "But Thorne's crazy about you. It was all over him that afternoon we played cards—every time he looked at you. Jake saw it, too. He mentioned it to me on the way home."

"Pure lust," she snapped. She caught Maggie's disturbed look and set her cup down suddenly. She put her hands over her face, shuddering. "I'm sorry. I've no right to burden you with all this. I'm in a bit of a state this morning. I'm sure you must think I'm insane, but just overlook it if you can."

"I don't think you're insane, dear, but I do think you're a very foolish young woman."

Rhea shook her head wearily. "Oh, I don't expect you to understand. Thorne has always been very nearly perfect in your eyes."

"Of course he isn't perfect!" Maggie snorted. "He's a man, isn't he?" Her gaze ran over Rhea slumped forlornly in a corner of the couch. Rhea's hands, which were trying to replace errant strands of black hair behind falling combs, were shaking visibly. "What you need is something a little stronger than tea."

Rhea struggled with a strong desire to cry. Biting her bottom lip, she said shakily, "Why, Maggie, I didn't know you allowed spirits in your house."

"I keep a little for cooking and medicinal purposes," Maggie said as she got to her feet. "There's a bit of brandy left from Christmas."

"Thank you. Yes, I think I could use something to steady my nerves."

Maggie brought the brandy in a juice glass and gave it to Rhea, who held the small glass in both hands as she lifted it to her mouth.

"Feeling better?" Maggie inquired after a moment.

Rhea nodded. "I think so. I'll just sit here another few minutes, and then I'll go and quit glooming all over you."

"You know I'm willing to listen any time, but Thorne is the one you have to talk to. I think you've just assumed your feelings for him aren't returned in kind. He should at least have a chance to confirm or deny that."

The brandy was warming her, stilling the shaking in her hands. Rhea felt calmer now, the ache lessened a little. "You're very kind, Maggie, but I can't see what would be accomplished by talking this over with Thorne. There have been other women. He admitted it to me. I'm not sure I can ever fully forgive him for that or if I could believe in him as utterly as I once did."

Maggie's head wagged disconsolately. "Only the young can be so self-righteous."

Rhea felt the tears at the back of her eyes. "That isn't fair. It's not self-righteousness—"

Maggie looked at her wryly. "Yes, it is, honey. I know because I once felt exactly as you are feeling now."

"You, Maggie?" Rhea made a sound of disbelief. "I can't believe that Jake ever gave you one second's worth of unhappiness."

"Oh, my dear, what idyllic notions you have. Every marriage has its problems, at one time or another." She studied Rhea's face for a long moment, then drew a deep breath, as if she had come to a decision. "I'm going to tell you something I've never told anyone, not my children, not even my favorite sister."

Maggie's tone was so earnest that Rhea leaned forward, waiting in silence for the other woman to go on. "When Jake and I had been married about three years—before I was pregnant with our first son—he was attracted to another woman. He was working in a sawmill near Poteau. He had lunch in the little café where the girl worked as a waitress, and that's how they met. There was an affair. I didn't know about it for weeks, and when I found out I was so hurt and humiliated—well, I just wanted to die. Oh, how I hated that girl—and Jake, too!"

"Oh, Maggie, you needn't go on—"

"But I want to. It's all right, dear. I've been able to think of it dispassionately for years. It's almost as if it happened to somebody else. But *then*—oh, then, I thought my life was ruined forever. I packed my suitcase and when Jake came home from work I threw it all in his face, told him I was leaving and that I never wanted to see him again. Well, we had a dinger of a fight then. He regretted what had happened, I could see that, even though it didn't make me feel any better. Jake told me he loved me, that the girl hadn't meant anything really, but that he wasn't going to take *all* the blame."

"He blamed you?" Rhea asked in surprise.

"Well, I wasn't perfect, either. I'd been trying to get pregnant for two years and couldn't—probably because I was so anxious and intense about it—and I'd reached a point where that's just about all I thought about. I brooded and was often depressed and convinced I would never have children. Jake said I'd become so obsessed with having a baby that I'd shut him out. Somehow I'd given him the impression that I thought it was his fault, that he wasn't as much of a man as he ought to be. He just went on and on. Things poured out of him that I'd never suspected he felt. And I had my say, too. Oh, it was quite a revelation—for both of us."

"But you didn't leave?"

"No. Jake asked me to give him another chance, promised it would never happen again. So I stayed, but I didn't forgive him, not for a long, long time. Every time we had a disagreement, I threw it up to him."

Rhea said doubtfully, "I can't even imagine you and Jake having a serious argument."

"Goodness knows we had our share in those first years. But finally I threw that girl up to Jake once too often."

"What did he do?"

"He sat me down and looked me in the eye and said, 'Maggie, I think we better settle something right here and now. Do you mean to go on punishing me the rest of my life for one mistake? Because if you do, maybe we better re-evaluate this marriage. Maybe it's not worth saving.' The upshot of it was that I never mentioned Jake's mistake again—but, of course, I thought about it from time to time, and it still hurt."

Rhea understood how difficult it must have been for Maggie to forget. "But you did get over it?"

"Our boys came along—a year apart—and I was too busy to spend much time feeling sorry for myself. Then our daughter was born. I remember being in the hospital after having Darlene. They wouldn't let the boys visit on the maternity ward, so Jake brought them to my window and let them watch me feed the baby. I was sitting in a chair, holding the baby, and watching the boys' curious little faces pressed against the glass, so wide-eyed, and Jake just beaming with pride. And I said to myself, 'Maggie, how could you have ever thought of leaving Jake and missing this?' It was one of those moments of revelation you hear about people having. It just hit me, 'Merciful heaven, I almost threw this all away—these precious children and that good, loving man.'"

When Maggie stopped talking, the silence seemed to Rhea to throb with possibilities, with roads not taken. Then Maggie leaned forward and touched her hand lightly. "Life isn't a fairy tale, honey, and men and women aren't Prince Charmings and Sleeping Beauties. If that were the case, I've no doubt we'd all become bored by the perfection of it in no time."

Rhea nodded, her head down, and Maggie said, "You and Thorne had something special. Talk to him. Go on your knees to him if you have to, but don't let him go without a fight."

Rhea moved to hug the older woman. Then she got quickly to her feet. "Thank you, Maggie. You've given me a lot to think about."

The walk back to the cabin was made in a different mood than the earlier walk to the Sinclairs'. Instead of dwelling on Thorne's shortcomings, Rhea began to examine her own. There was a basic insecurity in her nature that had made her always ready to believe the worst. Perhaps subconsciously she had never quite believed that she deserved as much happiness as she had had with Thorne in the beginning. It had never seemed quite possible that a man like Thorne Folsom could love someone like her. So when Diane Lowery had come out of Thorne's bedroom that night in New York, she had never doubted that he had been unfaithful to her. It was almost as if she had been expecting something terrible to happen. She hadn't given him a chance to explain. She had believed a casual acquaintance rather than her own husband. Was it any wonder that he had been angry and hurt? With Thorne it had been pride, rather than low self-esteem, that had gotten in his way. But as Maggie said, men and women were flawed creatures.

She was walking with her head down, absorbed in thought, and consequently wasn't aware of the activity at the cabin until she heard the laboring of a truck motor. It was the wrecker, toiling around the bend with her car in tow. The rented truck Thorne had driven already sat near the front steps. Thorne was standing on the porch, and when Rhea's car had been disengaged from the tow bar and left next to the truck, he paid the driver and, as the wrecker drove away, lifted his head to watch Rhea's approach.

"The hostages are freed," he commented dryly and, as she reached the steps, turned and went back into the cabin.

Rhea followed to find him gathering up his writing materials and tucking them into his suitcase, which lay open on the hearth. He didn't look up. She removed her coat and gloves and walked to the fireplace.

"I didn't realize we were hostages," she ventured.

"I meant in the Baconian sense—hostages to fortune."

"That applies to every human being who ever lived, doesn't it?" He shrugged and her gaze slid to the suitcase. "What are you doing?"

"Why," he inquired with a crooked little smile, "do women have such a tendency to ask questions with obvious answers?" He closed the suitcase and snapped the locks. He straightened and looked directly into her eyes for the first time.

His dark gaze brooded on her face, as if she were a chance-met stranger and he was trying to remember if he had seen her before. Emotion swelled up in her, threatening to overcome her—sorrow and regret and love too lightly taken and too easily cast aside. "Maybe—maybe they are only trying to fill up the silence."

He reached for his sheepskin jacket, which lay across the back of an armchair. Putting it on, he asked, "Well, is everything squared away with Cragmont? Did he kick up much of a fuss when he learned I was here? Or didn't you tell him?"

"I told him." She felt a chill and hugged herself. He was buttoning his coat and did not respond. She went on shakily, "I want you to know something. Don is only a friend, a good friend but nothing more."

He grew quite still, looking at her with hooded eyes. "Are you saying Cragmont never had you?"

"Yes—I mean, no, he hasn't. Nor has any other man. Only you."

He took a step toward her. "Is that true, Rhea? You wouldn't lie to me about a thing like this?"

She shook her head, her throat tightening. "It's true."

"Why?" he demanded, his tone uncertain, yet somehow unyielding.

Why? She stared at him, bewildered by the unbending stance of his body and the coolness in his voice. Didn't he know that she couldn't stand the thought of another man's touching her because she loved *him*? The admission trembled behind her quivering lips and she turned away from him to stare into the fire. "I—I guess I didn't want to be hurt again."

There was a long moment of silence, and then from the corner of her eye she saw him lift the suitcase. "I'll be at Gracie's until I can make other arrangements."

She turned to watch unbelievingly as he walked toward the door. He was actually going to leave! "Thorne," she said huskily, "I don't want you to go."

He turned around. There was an expression of confusion, almost of anger, on his face. His lips were white. "What are you trying to do now? You've hardly made a secret of wanting me out of here from the moment I arrived."

She stood there with pain tearing through her, pulsing in her veins. "I'm sorry," she muttered half under her breath.

"I know," he said heavily. "You're sorry, I'm sorry. We've apologized and apologized. Now you say you don't want me to go. But I can't stay here and be tormented any longer, Rhea. I thought being separated from you was the most painful thing possible, but I've found that being near you when you don't want me there is much worse."

"Is that how you feel?" she said. "Well, now you know how I feel, how I've felt for years."

He looked at her blankly. "What?"

She wanted to run to him, to fling herself in front of the door. It would be a rending relief to admit that she loved him, had always loved him. She was so tired of fighting to hide the way she felt. She looked at him with eyes filled with love and resentment and Thorne said urgently, "Maybe I'm dense, but you'll have to explain what you mean."

Her throat felt too tight with conflicting emotions to answer immediately. Thorne bent to set his suitcase on the floor. He walked toward her slowly. "It's too late for anything but honesty between us, Rhea. Do you have any idea what it's been like for me these past few days, thinking that you and Cragmont were lovers? Don't you understand how it tears me apart to think of another man near you, touching you?"

The harshness in the words got through to her. She looked searchingly up into his strained face. "I don't want a divorce," she murmured tremblingly. "I'll do whatever you want. I'll quit my job and we can stay here while you finish your book. I—I want to forget the past. For the first time I think that might be possible. I want a chance to win back your love. I love you, Thorne—I have never stopped loving you."

Thorne's hard mouth lifted in a quick smile, and then he reached out for her, hauling her into his arms, pressing her head against his shoulder with his hand. "You little fool," he said roughly. "Do you really think you have to win back my love? You never lost it. I thought that was obvious, I didn't think I had to tell you. Since you left me I haven't been able to look at another woman without thinking of you, remembering how you felt in my arms, wanting you so desperately. There will never be anyone but you for me. Do you want me to take a blood oath on it?" His hand smoothed the hair away from her face, lifted her chin so that he could look into her eyes. "Tell me again, Rhea. I have to hear you say it once more before I can start·to believe it."

Her brown eyes deepened to a rich black as she whispered the words he wanted to hear. "I love you, utterly, hopelessly, Thorne Folsom." She put her arms around his neck and bent his head to hers. Their lips touched in a long, yearning kiss. As she pulled her lips reluctantly from his, she said, "Take me to bed, husband."

He caught his breath and then smiled down at her teasingly. "I thought you don't approve of solving problems in bed." His voice was unsteady.

"What problems?"

Moments later they lay together, their naked bodies warm and pulsing with love and need. Thorne held his passion on a taut rein as his fingers and lips turned her body to molten fire. She quivered with a quaking need that was driving her to distraction. Tears of joy slipped down her cheeks.

"Thorne, I love you," she cried, pulling him down to cover her body, squirming to fit her soft curves more tightly to the hard length of his body, wanting to feel every inch of him pressing her down. She buried her face in his neck and heard the deep drumbeats of his heart.

He lifted his head to look deeply into her face, and she was profoundly moved to see the glitter of tears in his eyes. Erupting emotions shuddered through him as he took her with a flaming passion that leaped up to consume them both. And at the height of their pleasure he gasped out, "Yes, my darling—oh, yes!"

Later, wrapped in his arms, sated and exalted, her

fingers delicately traced the adored outlines of his face. "I haven't been taking any precautions," she murmured drowsily. "We might have started a baby already. What would you think about that?"

Thorne caressed her bare shoulder with his fingers. "I'd think we should build a nursery onto the cabin. In fact, we probably ought to get started on it right away. The chances of your becoming pregnant are going to be very high." His dreaming voice sounded sleepy and utterly satisfied. His hand slipped down to the warm fullness of her breast. "Give me a few minutes, and I'll show you what I mean."

Rhea smiled, her eyes closed. "Whatever you say, darling," she sighed, snuggling closer, entwining her body with his.

LOOK FOR NEXT MONTH'S
CANDLELIGHT ECSTASY ROMANCES™:

From the bestselling author of
Loving, The Promise, and Palomino

The RING

Danielle Steel

A DELL BOOK
$3.50   (17386-8)

A magnificent novel that spans this century's most
dramatic years, *The Ring* is the unforgettable story
of families driven apart by passion—and brought
together by enduring compassion and love.

Love—the way you want it!

Candlelight Romances

Dell Bestsellers

- ☐ **WHEN THE WIND BLOWS** by John Saul $3.25 (19857-7)
- ☐ **THY NEIGHBOR'S WIFE** by Gay Talese $3.95 (18689-7)
- ☐ **THE CRADLE WILL FALL**
  by Mary Higgins Clark $3.50 (11476-4)
- ☐ **RANDOM WINDS** by Belva Plain $3.50 (17158-X)
- ☐ **THE TRAITORS** by William Stuart Long $3.50 (18131-3)
- ☐ **BLOOD RED WIND** by Laurence Delaney ..$2.95 (10714-8)
- ☐ **LITTLE GLORIA . . . HAPPY AT LAST**
  by Barbara Goldsmith $3.50 (15109-0)
- ☐ **GYPSY FIRES** by Marianne Harvey $2.95 (12860-9)
- ☐ **NUMBER 1**
  by Billy Martin and Peter Golenbock $3.25 (16229-7)
- ☐ **FATHER'S DAYS** by Katherine Brady $2.95 (12475-1)
- ☐ **RIDE OUT THE STORM** by Aleen Malcolm ..$2.95 (17399-X)
- ☐ **A WOMAN OF TEXAS** by R.T. Stevens $2.95 (19555-1)
- ☐ **CHANGE OF HEART** by Sally Mandel $2.95 (11355-5)
- ☐ **THE WILD ONE** by Marianne Harvey $2.95 (19207-2)
- ☐ **THE PROUD HUNTER** by Marianne Harvey..$3.25 (17098-2)
- ☐ **SUFFER THE CHILDREN** by John Saul $2.95 (18293-X)
- ☐ **CRY FOR THE STRANGERS** by John Saul ..$2.95 (11870-0)
- ☐ **COMES THE BLIND FURY** by John Saul $2.75 (11428-4)
- ☐ **THE FLOWERS OF THE FIELD**
  by Sarah Harrison $3.50 (12584-7)

At your local bookstore or use this handy coupon for ordering:

Dell **DELL BOOKS**
P.O. BOX 1000, PINE BROOK, N.J. 07058

Please send me the books I have checked above. I am enclosing $_____
including 75¢ for the first book, 25¢ for each additional book up to $1.50 maximum
postage and handling charge.
Please send check or money order—no cash or C.O.D.s. Please allow up to 8 weeks for
delivery.

Mr./Mrs. _____

Address _____

City _____ State/Zip _____

Candlelight Ecstasy Romances

Bestsellers